GOATSONG

BY

PATRICIA DAMERY

Jan —
Much love, — + Gratitode!
Patricia

il piccolo editions
by

Goatsong

Copyright © 2012 Patricia Damery

ISBN 978-1-926715-76-6 Paperback

ISBN 978-1-926715-79-7 eBook

First Edition

Published simultaneously in Canada, the United Kingdom, and the United States of America. For information on obtaining permission for use of material from this work, please submit a written request to:

permissions@fisherkingpress.com

Fisher King Press
PO Box 222321
Carmel, CA 93922
www.fisherkingpress.com
+1-831-238-7799

GOATSONG

FOR YOU, STACEY

HOW THE GOAT WOMEN BROUGHT
ME INTO LIFE

I was ten years old when I first heard the Goatsong. That was when my life really began. Each time I've told you the stories of that year, I've relived the events, bittersweet as they were. Each retelling has brought renewed acceptance — and gratitude, for it was that year I was graced with the beauty of love.

Nelda told me that you have to be about the age I was then to hear the Goatsong. She told me the word *goatsong* is the Greek word for "tragedy": *tragos,* meaning "goat" and *oida,* meaning "song", *tragōidia.* Goatsong is the mysterious combination of humility and that essential ability to climb above, like a goat, or a song! To know the Goatsong of tragedy, Nelda told me, is to be reborn.

These stories are the ones you asked for over and over, the ones I told you during our years together. I understand why you loved them so much—each retelling has helped to heal *me*. I think they brought meaning to your own uprooted young life.

So, at your request, here is a last telling: your questions, my answers—how the Goat Women brought me into life.

YOUR QUESTIONS;
MY ANSWERS.

1

SOPHIA, TELL ME AGAIN ABOUT WHEN YOU MET THE GOAT WOMEN.

I was still living with Ma in the little town of Huckleberry on the Russian River when I met them. Because she worked evenings and nights, waitressing at the all-night diner, Ma didn't want me making noise during the day while she slept, so I left the house and did all kinds of things most kids would not have the opportunity to indulge in, you might say.

Huckleberry was full of people like Ma and me who were living on the edge — or falling off it. Many years before it had been a resort town, so the houses were really summer cabins, most of them built right along the river. This was great in the summer, because it didn't rain from April until October, and you were within yards of the thick, green river that was smooth enough to skip stones clear across and shallow enough to not fear drowning as you floated languidly along that watery corridor through redwoods and sandbars toward the sea. But winter was different. The water became muddy brown and turbulent then and sometimes swelled into the town, flooding many of the houses. Still, these cabins were cheap to rent, just right for Ma, who couldn't afford the higher-ground variety.

The summer morning I met Nelda was already hot before the sun even hit the tips of the redwoods across the river. I decided to follow the trail up the mountain behind our house and wade in the cool pool of the year-round spring near the top. I knew the animal trails and streambeds of that mountain like most kids know their backyards, so I started the long climb up the mountain even before the shafts of sunlight hit the forest floor.

I made fast progress. Most of the lower reach of the mountain was covered with the tall but youthful presence of second growth redwood, and after ten minutes or so, the smooth, bronze curves of madrone branches and trunks. The trail welcomed me, and I hummed to myself as I scanned the forest floor for the sour, four-leafed clover-like leaf I liked to suck on that I'd later identify as redwood sorrel and, in a sunny patch, the bright orange trumpets of sticky monkey flower.

I knew the seasons by the shapes and scents of their flowers. June brought the end of the spring wildflowers, but sometimes in the cooler and darker places you still found an arch of the tiny white blossoms of Solomon's Seal or, in a protected area, a delicate-tongued calypso orchid.

As I climbed the trail, the fragrance of bay laurel signaled that I was entering the level of vegetation where oak and bay thrived. I hummed a hello song, and then there was the excited rattle of a breeze in the thick, curved leaves of the coastal live oak. I knew the song of the wind in the foliage of each tree—the whisper and hush in the bay, the roar of gales in the tops of redwoods and fir. Sometimes I feel that I was raised mostly by those trees—at least until I met the Goat Women.

As I reached the spring where I wanted to swim, I saw that a large, sturdy-looking woman had already arrived. Her dark brown hair was short, and she wore jeans rolled up to her knees. Several small goats drank from the pool's cool, fresh water.

I had been all over that mountain a hundred times, but I had never come across this woman and her goats. I had heard about her, however. There were rumors about a Goat Woman, with legs as hairy as her goats', who sometimes let out sudden shrieks in the woods, shrieks that had curdled cream at Jimmy Maison's grandmother's house, so the rumor went. It was said that she danced in the meadows, and that goats would dance about her on their hind legs to the tinkling of invisible bells.

The woman sat on a rock, soaking her bare feet in the water. I watched from behind a stand of scotch broom as she ran a hand along one of the black goat's back. "Ah, Boris!" she said. "Your coat is so thick and shiny. The spring grass is showing itself." And the little goat with its eight-inch horns turned to her, mesmerized by her touch and soft voice. His feather duster tail wriggled wildly as her hand smoothed his hair.

"And Hornsby," she continued, pulling a foxtail from her own hair, "you, too. You are fatter and stronger from the spring greens. Such a beautiful coat you have!" Hornsby did not lift his head from drinking, but he also did not pull away from her touch. She settled back onto the rock and began humming a song I had never heard. Her eyes closed. A moment later the humming stopped and she sat still, listening.

"Okay, who's there?" she said, a little sternly.

I was startled and remained quiet.

She opened her eyes. "You," she said, staring directly at the scotch broom. "Do you think that I don't see you?"

Her voice was soft, I remember that, even when she raised it. There was a music to her words. Nevertheless, I could not breathe as she continued staring in my direction. I tried to see if she had hairy legs, but I couldn't tell. The goats were wary now and hovered closer to the woman. The one she called Hornsby rested the top of his head against her forearm. Boris stepped behind her. The remaining goats all stood at alert, looking in my direction, as the woman did. The hair stood straight up in a ridge along the middle of their backs, making them look twice their size.

We all stayed frozen this way a long time. The woman did not say another word, nor did she move. Neither did I— until I couldn't stand it any more. I had to move my foot to keep it from going to sleep and stepped on a twig that broke.

"Come on out of there," she said.

I bent over and peeked nervously out from behind the bush. She was still sitting there, leaning back against a bay tree, looking directly at me. She smiled, and I slowly straightened up.

"So there you are."

I said nothing, because I didn't know what to say.

"The cat got your tongue?" she chided.

"No," I said, recovering myself a little. "Who are you?"

"Nelda," she answered. "And who are you?"

"Sophie. My real name is Sophia, but everyone calls me Sophie, because that's easier to say, and because not too many kids are called Sophia."

She studied me in a way I wasn't used to. "The name suits you."

We continued staring at each other. "What are you doing here?" I blurted out.

Nelda smiled her warm smile again, and I stepped a bit closer. She sat up a little. "Resting," she said. "Getting some water for the goats. May I ask you the same?"

"This is where I go when it's hot."

"I've never seen you here," Nelda said.

"Well, you just haven't been here when I was." I paused a moment. "Are you the Goat Woman?"

Nelda laughed, the sound like clear notes played on some sort of a flute. "I do *have* goats," she answered.

"Do you have hairy legs?" I pushed.

"What?" She smiled, then pulled a pant leg well up over her knee and extended her leg toward me. I took a few more steps forward and glanced quickly at it. Nothing too spectacular, I thought. I mean, maybe she didn't shave, but she didn't have goat legs, either.

"Sorry, I just needed to know," I said. "There's a story about a Goat Woman. I thought that it might be you."

She smiled again. Her eyes were as blue as forget-me-nots. "Well, it's possible that I am she. Not many people keep goats, though I'll never know why. And you know, when people do something a little different, all kinds of stories start flying around." She pulled her pant legs back down. "Where do you live, anyway?" she asked.

"Down the mountain."

"Does your mother know you're up here?"

"She doesn't care. She's sleeping because she works at night."

"Who takes care of you?"

"I take care of myself."

"I see," Nelda said. She stretched her legs out, crossing her feet at the ankles, and I found myself carefully examining them again.

I liked this woman who spoke so directly to me. I wasn't used to adults engaging me in conversation. Ma mostly scolded about what I had or hadn't done or gave orders about what I should do while she was gone.

I paused at the door of her room before I left the house each morning, allowing my eyes to adjust to the darkened room. Her waitress uniform always lay in a heap on the floor. If I made out two forms in bed, I would hightail it out of there, but if it was only Ma, I would pause a few moments and study the way her long black hair spilled over the pillow and onto the sheet.

People described my mother as being cute. Her nose turned up and she had dark eyes with a certain fire in them. She'd talk back to any trucker at the diner who had a smart mouth, and they seemed to like her even more for it.

Maybe this feistiness was one thing I got from her, but there wasn't much else. I didn't look like her. My hair was short and blond and very curly, and I knew I'd never work as a waitress in an all-night diner. That's one thing I'd never do.

Thinking these thoughts, I sat down beside Nelda. Boris immediately sniffed my hand, and I carefully reached out to pet his back. His hair was coarse and stiff, his lips soft as they searched my fingers for a treat.

"Here," Nelda said, pulling a broad-leafed weed from the ground beside her. "Give him this plantain. They love it."

Boris snatched the vertical veined leaf out of my hand, chewed a couple of times, and swallowed.

"You didn't chew very long!" I chided.

"He'll catch it later," Nelda said. "They are browsers. They pick, swallow, and then later, when they have a nice shady spot to rest in, they sit down, belch it up, and chew their cud."

I looked over at Hornsby, who was resting and chewing. His eyes were half closed, and he seemed to be smiling. Goats are pretty gross, I thought, but even looking at his lazy eyes, I began to relax.

So that is how I met Nelda, the first of the three.

I started looking for her each morning after I tiptoed out of the house, pretending I was tracking her just as I tracked the red deer that grazed the upper meadows and the coyote, so much more wily and hard to find. Then, whenever I saw

Nelda and her plump goats walking on the trail above the meadow, or refreshing themselves at the spring, or resting beside the fire road that crossed the mountain to Huckleberry, I watched them a while.

Nelda moved with such deliberation and grace. She was a substantial woman, not fat, but definitely not thin either. She kept her brown hair cut short, and she was about at that time of life when women become ageless. Not young, not old. Or maybe both, or either. You can't tell.

I liked her gentleness. The goats did, too, though they had a wild side even she couldn't tame. Sometimes they would leap into the air, butting each other, and Nelda would sternly say, "Now stop that this moment!" Maybe they would, and maybe they wouldn't. They were creatures of instinct, after all.

Once Hornsby had a big gash over his eye where Boris had wounded him, and Nelda dabbed an herbal salve on it that she made for such occasions. Hornsby waited patiently as she worked, and then he went out again to play his rough goat games with Boris. The female goats were not as likely to be butting like that. They were more into leading the pack. Nelda told me that the smallest goat, Natalie, was the queen goat. Her job was to lead and to find good vegetation for the herd to eat.

I soon learned that Nelda lived in an old cabin way up in the mountains above the town. She had only two rooms, a larger room in front that held a table, two chairs, and an old wood stove, and a smaller bedroom in the back. Outside, under a large oak, she had built a lean-to where the goats slept at night.

I was not used to seeing such simple accommodations. In town even the simple houses had several rooms, not two. No one would think of building a two-room cabin anymore. But Nelda told me that cabins used to be just that, and that materials had been used more sparingly and carefully in earlier times.

I started visiting often, and Nelda would always fix me tea from the minty-smelling herb that grew along the east side of her cabin, probably because that was the one plant the goats didn't like. I would sit at her table as she boiled the water while humming a song neither of us knew the words to. I listened to Nelda hum and watched her tear up the leaves of the mint to steep in the water as I chewed on a biscuit.

"Sure it's okay with your mother that you visit me so often?" she asked one morning. "Seems like you're here more than you are there these days."

"It's okay." I said. Nelda didn't understand that Ma was just too busy to be a mom. She never meant to become a mom, really. I was what happened when she got feisty with a truck driver once, or maybe it was a carpenter. In fact, the identity of my father was a question that my mother could never answer to my satisfaction. "Just so I'm out of the way, she's happy," I told Nelda.

"Do you have any brothers or sisters?"

"There's just me."

"I was the only child, too," Nelda said. "It can be lonely, being the only."

I nodded and noisily sipped the tea Nelda had placed in front of me. The enormous cup was chipped in two places around the rim. I stirred in three teaspoons of honey and sipped again. I often felt Nelda observing me, just as she did the goats, and my hair and eyes, too, soon grew shiny under her watchful eye. I must have grown three inches that summer she fed me potions of herbs, polenta, and goat cheese with honey.

One morning, Nelda invited me to walk with her to town. We followed the dirt road along the top of the ridge before it disappeared into the redwoods and then walked down to the valley. I was to sit with the goats in the meadow while Nelda went on to trade goat cheese and extra goat milk for the few staples she needed: whole wheat flour, coffee, Raisin Bran cereal, and black, red, and brown speckled beans she soaked and cooked with seasonings that smelled like magic potions. Sometimes she also bought a lime or lemon. The best part was the chocolate bar that she divided between us before our walk home.

As usual, the morning was hot. When we reached the meadow, I crawled under the starburst branches of a live oak that brushed the ground. The goats were hot, too, and crawled under the branches into the shade with me. I laid my head on Natalie's stomach, and Emily laid her head on me. The other goats slowly settled about us. The four male goats usually napped by themselves, and this morning they formed a group under the madrone just behind us.

I soon fell fast asleep, and the heat made my dreams chaotic and restless. Somewhere I heard a snorting that came closer and closer. I was running, and still the sound was gaining on me. All around me was brush and tangled vines. Still I ran, my arms scratched and stung by blackberry shoots and nettles. A tough vine caught my foot, and I fell forward, my eyes suddenly wide open.

I was glad to be out of the dream, but I could still hear the strange snorting sound. I sat up, peering out from my oak retreat. An old woman sat on a rock in the scattered shade, heaving with sobs. Beside her were a couple of shopping bags filled with clothing and blankets. She sat hunched over, her head on her knees. She had masses of faded red, curly hair that flared in a shining haze about her head. Her back heaved up and down as she gulped for air, moaning and wailing in the way only privacy allows. I watched her a long time.

The goats were alert but quiet. The hair on their backs stood up in straight ridges along their spines, of course, and they looked at me to see how I was reacting. In my mind I told them not to worry, that this was only an old woman. Finally the woman's crying quieted.

"What's wrong?" I asked a bit loudly, my curiosity about her display of grief too strong to suppress.

The woman jumped. "Who's there?" she barked, wheeling around to look for the source of the voice.

"It's me, Sophie." I crawled out from the shelter of the oak, the dried leaves crackling beneath my knees.

The old woman straightened her back, her face suddenly business-like, but I could see a kindness in her eyes. Only her damp and swollen face suggested she had been crying. "What are you doing, spying?"

"I'm not spying," I said. "My name's Sophie, and I'm waiting on Nelda. You woke me up with your crying. So what's wrong?"

"What makes you think that something's wrong?"

"Well, you were crying."

"No, I wasn't."

I sat down on the rock beside her, the goats still silent in the trees. A tear leaked from the old woman's eye and ran down her cheek. "See? There's a tear right there."

"Okay, okay," she conceded. "Why are you making such a big deal out of an old woman's tears?"

I shifted my weight on the rock we sat on, and the shopping bags brushed my leg. "What are you doing with all these bags of clothes?"

The old woman waved her hand dismissively. "Questions, questions, questions. It's nothing to concern you."

The goats were still in the shade, hiding. Or resting. It could be either. We could hear a motor grinding its way up the hill, now louder, now softer. After a few minutes, a white Toyota pickup rounded the corner. The old woman was suddenly on her feet, walking toward it. Although she was plump, she walked with an authority that could call anyone up short. The driver, a young, close-shaven man, slowed and stopped.

"Haven't seen a black lab up here, have you?" he asked.

"Certainly haven't," the woman answered. She stood looking into the bed of the pickup, which was partially covered with a blue tarp, and this seemed to make the man nervous.

"Let me know if you see him," the man said, looking straight ahead, and he hurriedly drove off.

"One two four ADR. Girl," she said, turning to me, "help me remember that number." She fetched a notebook and pencil out of her pocket, all the time repeating the number to herself. "One two four ADR. One two four ADR." She then scribbled on the paper. "Yeah, I'll let you know if I see anything," she said sarcastically, staring toward the fading cloud of dust.

"What are you doing?" I asked.

"People dump up here," she said. "I want it stopped, but the police can't do nothing about it."

"Oh," I said.

"You going to be here a little while?" she asked. "I'm going to walk up the road and see if I can see anything. Watch my bags, would you?"

"Sure," I answered. But she had already begun to walk quickly up the dirt road into the dust cloud that was only beginning to fade. "Wait!" I called. "I don't know your name. "

"Dee," she called. "Dee Williams. I'll be back in a while."

I waited a while—a long while. The goats stayed in the shade, dozing and chewing, chewing and dozing. I drew circles in the dust with a piece of willow that I had brought down from the creek, spelling my name, then Nelda's, then Hornsby's. It was getting hotter, and I was thirsty. The names of all the goats were written in the dust before I heard

Nelda's humming coming up the dirt road. The goats heard it, too, of course. Boris stood up and let out a loud "Baaaaa!" They all stood up, but stayed put in the shade under the oak.

"Took me longer than I thought," Nelda said. She had on a backpack and carried two large paper sacks. She slowed when she saw the shopping bags sitting beside me and looked at me quizzically.

"Dee's," I said. "I'm watching them for her while she runs after the truck that was going to dump garbage on the mountain."

"Who's Dee?"

"An old woman. I was sleeping, and when I woke up, she was sitting here, crying. She never told me why. And then this pickup came by. The guy said he was looking for his dog, but he had a bunch of junk in the back of the pickup, and Dee thought he was going to dump it, so she went to see."

"And you're watching her bags?"

"She asked me to. She said she would be back in a while."

At this exact point Dee rounded the corner. "Just what I thought!" she shouted triumphantly. "A big pile of fresh garbage up the road a couple bends. But this time I got some junk mail with his name and address. Now those deputies will have something to go on."

She slowed as she got to the spot where we were sitting and saw Nelda. "Hello," she said, suddenly a little reserved. And to me, "I'll take those bags now."

"No wait!" I said as she hurriedly leaned down to pick up the shopping bags by their tattered handles. "You haven't met Nelda! "

Dee was wary as she looked first at the goats — who were now all out in plain sight, munching madrone leaves — and then at Nelda. Nelda smiled at Dee. "Sophia here was watching the goats while I was in town doing some shopping," she said, stroking Natalie, who stood beside her. Then she stroked Emily, then Boris. As her hand ran along the ridge of each back, the hair shrank. Boris, Hornsby, Tarquin, then Natalie, Emily. It was important to greet each goat in this order, so none of them got upset.

As Nelda kept greeting and reassuring the goats, she glanced at Dee casually. "So you found someone dumping. Certainly is a lot of it on this road up here. Everyone in town seems to think this is a great place to dump garbage."

"Well, I think something needs to be done about it, and I can't seem to get the deputies to do anything. They would rather be doing their shooting practice on the ridge, or drinking coffee down at the diner. Garbage is of no concern to them. But this time I got some evidence." She pulled several envelopes from her pocket. "Look, every single one of these has the same name and address. I also have the license number of the truck. Now all I have to do is see if that pickup is parked at this address, and then we'll have him."

"Where do you live, Dee?" I thought the moment that those words were out of my mouth that it might have been rude to ask. There was a considerable silence, then Dee said, "Well, had you asked me last week, I could have told you. I might not have, but I could have. Now I'll have to take a rain check."

"What's a rain check?" I asked.

"It means another time. I am looking for another address."

"But where do you sleep?"

"It depends," she said, somewhat cautiously.

"Sophie, you're sure full of questions," Nelda said. "Let's give Dee a break. She's got enough questions without ours too."

"No, it's alright," Dee said. "Actually, it's refreshing to have someone care enough to ask. Most of the time, people don't want to know. I was living in a house that burned down last Thursday night. People say vagrants started a fire on the floor and burned the house down, but I know that a neighbor burned it down because he didn't want an abandoned house nearby with an old woman—or two—living out back. I escaped with just these two bags of stuff. So," she said, turning to me, "those are the grisly details, Sophie. And I am now looking for another residence."

We were all silent for a bit, then Nelda said, "I'm sorry." Dee nodded her head.

"Nelda," I said. "Did you get the chocolate bar?"

"Sure did," she nodded.

"I bet we could divide it three ways."

Nelda smiled. "I bet we could, too. Let's all have a seat in the shade."

TELL ME ABOUT WHEN YOU MET ESTER.

Ester was different. People said she was senile, but I think she had always been that way. She wasn't senile and she wasn't crazy, either. In fact, she was saner than most.

She was really old when I first met her. Dee had befriended Ester the winter the river flooded even the post office, and it turned out she had been squatting with Dee when that house burned down. Dee was like that, always helping somebody out.

So it went like this: shortly after we met Dee on Huckleberry Mountain, Nelda offered to let her live at the cabin until she could find another arrangement. Dee told Nelda that there was one complication, that she had a responsibility, and Nelda said she was sure that could be managed, having no idea about what—or who—that responsibility was. One morning when I went up to Nelda's cabin, she was trimming the goats' hooves, and Dee was sweeping the tiny porch. And there, seated in a rocker in a pool of morning sun, was someone else, the tiniest, boniest woman I ever saw in my life. Even though the morning was warm, Ester wore a brown wool coat and thick cotton stockings. She looked more like a wren than a person, but it turned out she wasn't nearly as nimble as a bird. In fact, Ester moved so slowly and carefully that I wondered how she ever made it up and down the mountain.

She had all the time in the world, of course. Not that the rest of us don't! We just think we don't. But Ester moved like one of those banana slugs that lived in the redwoods, and she missed very little. The first day I met Ester, Dee suggested we accompany her to get her social security check at the post office and then her food stamps at social services. I didn't usually go into town, because I personally liked staying as invisible as possible. Maybe once you're invisible to someone, like I felt I was to my mom, you're most comfortable staying that way everywhere. But when Dee asked if I would like to accompany Ester and her, I said I would, always being up for something new. Nelda said she had some logs to split, and that I might as well go ahead with the other two, because I would just be bored if I stayed with her.

We started off walking the fire road that runs the ridge. Below we could see a fog, like a white wooly worm crawling up the river channel. Ospreys flapped happily in the morning air currents and spikes of redwoods punched through the fog toward the clearest blue. I skipped ahead, and then back to join the two old women, then ahead and back again, as they slowly made their way along the rutted road.

As long as you looked up or out, the view was beautiful. But if you looked down, you saw the stained sofas and rusted refrigerators and cars littered around, and mounds of garbage that people had been dumping there for years.

About ten minutes out, Ester stopped and walked to the edge of the road. "We got to keep going," Dee said. "It's going to get too hot to get back up here if we don't keep moving."

Ester stood, staring into the brush below. Then she pulled a notebook out of her pocket, along with a small pencil. She was scribbling on the pad and mumbling under her breath when I skipped up. "Three gallon jugs, empty, Coke, 7up, one label too torn to read," she said as she scribbled.

"What are you doing, Ester?"

"She's logging garbage!" Dee snapped. "Damn! Sometimes I think she's as crazy as a coot."

"Empty smashed package of Marlboro cigarettes. Half gallon milk carton, flattened."

"But why is she logging garbage?"

"She has her reasons, but they're not reasons most of us understand." Dee was beginning to steam like she had that day she had chased the pickup. "She's done it for as long as I've known her."

"Four smashed aluminum Pepsi cans, five Budweiser cans...." Ester continued in her monotone voice. She seemed to be in another world, no longer aware of Dee and me. "Three used paper diapers, four letters, crumpled, one Pacific Bell bill."

"Ester, damn it, don't do this to us now. We have got to go." Dee pulled her arm, but Ester continued, oblivious. Dee didn't persist.

"One car chassis, indistinguishable brand, indistinguishable color, rusted."

"What are the reasons the rest of us don't understand?," I persisted, directing my question to Ester this time.

Ester stopped. She stared a moment longer down the hill, then tore the piece of paper from her tablet and handed it to me. She dug in her other pocket a moment and then handed me a small thumbtack. "Honey, would you crawl down the hill and tack this to the tree by that pile?" she asked.

I took the paper and the tack and slid down the steep slope a few feet to the tree. Listed were the contents of the pile as Ester had spoken them:

3 empty soft drink bottles, Coke, 7up, one label
  too worn to read

empty smashed package Marlboro cigarettes

4 smashed aluminum Pepsi cans

5 Budweiser cans

3 used paper diapers

4 letters, crumpled

1 Telephone bill

1 car chassis, indistinguishable brand, indistinguishable color, rusted

I tacked the paper to the tree. "Ester, why are you doing this?" I asked.

"So people know what has been dumped here," she said simply.

"But why write it down? Anyone can see. You don't need to make a list and post it." I crawled back up the slope and brushed off my bare knees.

Ester began to walk slowly toward town. "Why do you think people dump? They're getting rid of stuff. They've used what they want, and they want to be rid of the rest. They never want to see the stuff again."

"But *we* see it," Dee added. "Every time we walk along here, we see it. Someone needs to clean this up. Remind me, Girl—she often called me that—to stop by the police station while we're in town to check on their progress with the license number I gave them the other day."

"Maybe we can clean it up," I offered.

"Cleaning it up isn't going to help," Ester said.

"It would damn well make the place look better!" Dee sputtered.

"Only for a while," Ester said. "Do you think people are going to quit dumping?"

"But what *will* help?" I asked.

"*Seeing* what is thrown away," Ester said.

"*Umph!*" Dee snorted. "We live here; this is our land. Our job is to keep it cleaned up."

"That'll do no good," Ester said quietly. "It's little different from throwing something out. Either way, it is not seen. That's *my* job. *Seeing* it."

Dee mumbled something. Now I wasn't skipping. Instead, I walked carefully between them, pacing myself to match their steps. An osprey circled, peeping forcefully.

It felt strange to be walking with grown-ups like that. I never went anywhere with my mother, and there were no other adults I spent time with before the Goat Women. I liked it, even though it meant walking as if I were in molasses.

In time, we made it to town. When we reached the first houses, Dee straightened my hair. I stood completely still as she combed it with her fingers, feeling her hand on every hair of my head. "There now," she said, holding my face with both hands when she was done. "You don't look so much like an urchin!"

As we passed the shops, Dee looked in the windows as Ester inspected the gutters. I walked in between. We stopped at the police station first.

"Young man," Dee greeted the deputy who was sitting behind the window of the substation. "I've come to check your progress on the garbage I reported on Huckleberry Mountain."

"When was the report made?"

"Two weeks ago Friday. I gave you several pieces of mail with the name and address of the man whose truck dumped the garbage. I also gave you his license number."

The man disappeared into the back room. Ester began to walk slowly toward the wastebasket, but Dee stepped in between, suggesting that she have a seat on the bench.

The man returned a minute later and said, "We sent a deputy to the address, but the man moved."

"He didn't move the week after I brought in the license number and letters," Dee replied. "I walked by that address twice, and he was still there then."

"Sorry, ma'am, our coverage is minimal. There just aren't enough officers to answer everything."

"Why don't you just say that the road is the least of your worries."

"I wouldn't say the least. There're a lot of calls that have more priority, though."

Dee stared a long time at the young deputy, obviously angry. "Young man," she finally said, "one thing I've learned is people act a lot nicer in a clean house. If the house is trashed and unkempt, the people act unkempt too. If it's neat and lovingly cared for, people feel calmer. Maybe your most important priority should be keeping that road cleaned up so people who go up there act like people, not hoodlums. Maybe you have it backwards."

The man stared at Dee a second. I wasn't sure how he was taking the confrontation, and I felt nervous for a second. Then he laughed. "Interesting idea," he said, returning to his paper work. "But we can't spare the personnel for clean-up work."

Dee continued staring at the deputy. The deputy just continued writing, seemingly unaware of Dee's penetrating look.

Finally, I said, "Come on, Dee, let's go get the mail." I took her hand, and she jumped a little, surprised, I think, to feel it. Then I felt her fingers curl around my own.

"Okay, Sophie," she said. "Let's get Ester out of here before she sees anything in the dumpster." Ester was staring out the glass door toward the alley. Dee gently took her arm. "Let's go get your check," she said.

Dee went into the post office to get the check while Ester sat with me on the bench outside in the sun. When Dee returned, she had two envelopes, one with containing Ester's check, and the other with a postmark from Brighten, Massachusetts. "Do you know someone by the name of Wilton in Massachusetts?" she asked Ester.

"Wilton? Oh yes, that would be my niece and her husband."

"Well, here's a letter from them," Dee said. "Don't have my reading glasses, though. Sophia, could you read this for Ester?" She handed me the unopened envelope.

The letter was a single page on embossed paper. There was a light perfume smell as I opened it. "Dear Aunt Ester," – the handwriting was not easy to read – "Hope that you are doing well. We plan to arrive in San Francisco on July 2. Bill will be attending a … –I can't read this word."

"Spell it," Dee said.

"C-o-n-f-e-r-e …"

"Conference," Dee interjected.

"… a conference on helping p-r-o-f-e-s-s-i-o-n-a-l-s …"

"Professionals," Ester said. Dee did not even try.

"… and the aged. We will be in San Francisco during the week, but thought we would drive up and visit you on the following Saturday …"

"Oh my god," said Dee. Ester said nothing.

"Why 'Oh my god'?" I asked.

"Keep reading," Dee answered.

"We will be happy to help you with any errands that you may need to run, and will stay only for the day, driving back that evening. It will be so much fun to see you again after all these years. Your loving niece, Alice."

"Jesus Christ."

Ester said nothing.

"Jesus Christ," Dee said again. "They'll have you in a nursing home in no time."

Ester sat quietly, although alert. I sat down beside her. "Maybe you can use my mom's house," I said.

"Your mom wouldn't go along with that, Girl," Dee said. "She probably doesn't have the slightest idea you're hanging out with three strange women and a herd of goats. We don't need the county on us too … But you've given me an idea, by jigger!"

"What, Dee?" I loved her change of tone. I couldn't imagine what idea I had given her, and she wouldn't tell me any more right then. She said she needed to think about it before she explained.

Ester looked a little depressed, or was it resigned? She seemed content to leave things up to Dee. Sometimes when I've thought of Ester through the lens of the years, she has reminded me of a small, hunted animal that had accepted her destiny, as if she was, after all, just part of the food chain. She didn't reel against the flow of events like Dee and the rest of us did. She was simply waiting and recording everything she saw until fate caught up with her.

3

TELL ME ABOUT WHEN YOU STARTED LOGGING GARBAGE, TOO.

We couldn't go anywhere without having to stop and wait for Ester to log garbage, which took forever. The logical thing to do was to help her, so we could get where we were going quicker, wherever that was on a given day. By this time, I had begun to think of myself as living high on the ridge to the north of town. From up there, I could see the river curling through a deep canyon to the south before it reached the flood plain where the town had been built, and where I lived with Ma. We could see the river from almost anywhere along the fire road. Every time I looked at it, I remembered those times the river entered the town. TV cameras arrived to broadcast the story about the poor people being rescued by motorboats and then airlifted to the Red Cross shelter in the city several miles away.

The townspeople accepted this occasional flooding and probably shouldn't have. Outsiders have all kinds of ideas about that: that the town shouldn't have been built there at all; that federal funds were being wrongly used to let people in the flood plain rebuild; that these people were nutty anyway, so why worry much?

But the truth—and of course I didn't understand this for a long time—was that over the years the floods got worse and worse because of the people living upstream who had built so many buildings, roads, and parking lots that there was not enough ground left for the water to sink into. So all the rainwater just drained into the river, making it swell and flow faster, until it took up too much space in the little town on its way to the ocean. And then there was the issue of money. The ones flooded out were not the people who could afford the homes higher up the mountain, but people like Ma and me, poor people lucky enough to find the low rents at all, people who couldn't afford to think about moving. Where else could we go? So when the water rose into our living rooms and bedroom closets, wicking up the ties of our robes to saturate everything in the closet, we didn't call our senators to demand something get done upstream to change things. Instead, we partied together. It was the only way we could handle the prospect of losing everything. The people upstream watched our plight on the evening news and judged us: uneducated white trash, river rats.

Well, there is a larger picture. That's one thing Ester taught me by logging garbage.

Nelda was matter-of-fact about this logging. She just got down in the heaps with me, and we picked through the piles and called the contents up to Ester, who did the writing. At first, of course, Dee complained, like she always did, and then, in time, she gave up and started logging like the rest of us. It was the most expedient thing to do.

It was interesting, really. We stopped being so judgmental about those people who left their trash on the Huckleberry fire road. Nelda and I would make up stories about their lives, which wasn't very hard to do.

"One yellow Styrofoam plate, rectangular, coated with cheese sauce, chewed. One plastic container, mustard, squeezed. One large paper cup, Pepsi, plastic lid, one-tenth full, wouldn't you say, Sophie?"

I looked at the small pile there alongside the road as Ester scribbled.

"And one twelve-inch-square cellophane," I added. "Who was this, Nelda?"

"Oh, I imagine he came up here to get a breath of fresh air. He probably is a meter reader for PG and E, bought his lunch at the deli in town and drove up here to eat."

"Slob," Dee added. "Born in a barn! Doesn't know how to clean up after himself."

"Maybe he just accidentally dropped it here," I suggested.

"He may have absently dropped it here, but I don't think that it was accidental," Nelda said. "The man obviously is a city boy. Not born in a barn, Dee. If he were born in a barn, he wouldn't throw his trash in the countryside. Only city people are so oblivious to the country as to throw their lunch garbage on the roadside."

"Which is why I think they need a talking to," Dee answered, suddenly interested in joining us. She searched in and around the pile for any identifying information, but came up with nothing.

"One Budweiser can, empty, perfect condition," I called.

"He had a buddy with him," Dee said.

"Doubt his buddy would be drinking only a beer while he was having a main course and Pepsi," Nelda said. "Two different visits, two different individuals, I'd say."

Ester called to me to get the notes she had made and to pin them to the nearest tree above each pile. The goats were nearby, browsing on young snowberry shoots. As we all watched, Boris stood on his hind legs to reach the first note I pinned to a small oak and quickly ate it.

"My kind of goat," Dee said. "Not a litter bug."

Although Ester saw Boris eat the note, she said nothing. She just began to ever so slowly walk toward town. I pinned the next note higher on a tree, even though Boris showed no interest this time. He was back onto the snowberry shoots.

Dee was unusually silent as we started the descent into town, which meant that she was thinking. She muttered to herself, but it did no good to ask her what about, because she just waved us off.

"Why are you muttering, Dee?" I asked. "We can't hear you when you mutter."

"I don't mean for you to hear, or I wouldn't mutter," she said, annoyed. "I'm thinking."

"About what?" I pushed.

"Why are you always so full of questions, Girl? Can't you leave anything alone? I have to figure out how we are going to keep Ester out of the nursing home."

This silenced us all for a few minutes. Then I pressed again. "Would Ester get to log in the nursing home?"

"Girl, what questions! Of course not! Ester would be so doped up she wouldn't know a wastebasket from cooking pot. Not that she'd be around any cooking pots. She'd have frozen microwaved dinners prepared somewhere on the East Coast. No, Sophia, if Ester is going to keep on logging, we are going to have to keep her out of the nursing home." She turned to Nelda. "I can't believe I'm trying to devise a plan to keep Ester logging! Not to mention, walking around with a herd of goats!"

At this, Nelda noticed the goats were no longer with us. They were still back at the last garbage find. She called Natalie, and before we knew it, eight goats were running toward us, bells ringing wildly.

"I almost have the plan," Dee continued, "except for one thing. The plan involves both you and me, Nelda, which leaves the goats. Who is going to watch them for the afternoon?"

"Me!" I said. "I'll stay with them at the clearing. I stay with them all the time."

"For *all* afternoon?" Dee queried. "That's a long time."

"I like being with the goats a long time," I said.

Nelda was not so sure. "You've stayed with them for an hour or so, but never a whole afternoon."

"Please?" I begged. "Let me, *please*? Who else can do it?"

The women were silent. They knew there was no answer to that question. The silence was broken when Ester veered off to the right again. "Ester, you make me wonder if I'm out of my mind trying to keep you out of that place." Dee was exasperated. "This is too much! Come on! You're as crazy as a coot, and I am, too."

But Dee was gentle as she guided Ester to the center of the road, and Ester allowed herself to be steered away from the other possible dumping sites we passed. Her brown coat flapped around her calves. When I looked at Nelda, she smiled, but she looked worried. I felt pretty good, though, thinking that Dee had a good plan and that I would play an important part in it.

1 yellow Styrofoam plate, rectangular, coated with cheese sauce, chewed.

1 plastic container of mustard, squeezed.

1 large paper cup, Pepsi, 1/10 full.

Plastic lid.

Chapter 3

I twelve-inch-square of cellophane.

I Budweiser can, empty, perfect condition.

SOPHIA, TELL ME SOME OF THE STUFF YOU FOUND.

3 gallon jugs, empty, Coke, 7up, one label too torn to read

empty smashed package Marlboro cigarettes

½ gallon milk carton, flattened

~

2 beer cans, Budweiser, crushed

1 pint milk carton, empty, Clover chocolate, good condition

~

1 beer bottle, quart, Coors, empty

~

Chapter Four

6 one-gallon plastic milk cartons, Lucerne empty, excellent condition.

1 poncho, brown, torn at breast.

2 chlorine bleach bottles, label less, pristine white, excellent condition.

3 2-liter formula cans, empty, rusted.

1 plastic sheeting, gray, about 10 ft. x 12 ft., torn.

13 aluminum cans, 6 root beer, 7 Pepsi light, dented.

1 plastic sheet, clear, torn.

1 paperboard meat tray, blood stained.

1 aluminum beer can, Budweiser, smashed.

TELL ME ABOUT DEE AND
MOTORCYCLE MOUNTAIN.

If you followed the Huckleberry fire road past the place I first met Dee, you eventually ended up at the top of Motorcycle Mountain. The spot was spacious: a flattened, barren plateau that had never recovered from the turn-of-the-century clear-cut of the redwoods. From here you could see the ocean to the west and the tall, purple mountains to the east and south. Large, hollow stumps bordered the flattened area. Young men swirled trucks through the mud on this plateau during the wet winter months and used it for target practice during the dry season. Millions of gun shells littered the ground. Even the police spent a good deal of time here for target practice. So each time a large four-wheel-drive pickup zoomed past us as we walked Huckleberry, leaving us in a fog of earth, we knew where it was going.

One morning we decided to go by way of Motorcycle Mountain to a meadow on the other side of the ridge. Although the morning was cool and misty, you could tell by the golden restlessness of the fog that the sun was about to burn through. The hillside dropped a couple of hundred feet to the left and rose triumphantly through redwoods and bay trees to the right.

"This is our lucky day," Nelda said suddenly. "We are going to make it just in time."

"Just in time for what?" I asked.

"The raising of the wings," Nelda answered. "Remember the old fir up ahead that has lost so many of its lower branches? Turkey vultures gather there this time of morning. They wait high on the top branches until that splendid moment when the sun evaporates the fog."

"Wait for what?" I asked.

"You'll see. Now let's walk more quickly. We don't want to miss it."

Nelda and I started walking a little faster. Dee and Ester were not to be hurried. Nelda called to the goats, who were browsing on madrone leaves, and their bells tinkled more rapidly. Nelda told me once that she had strung the bells on the goats' collars because the clear ring of a bell on a goat made the fairies laugh.

So this morning I called to Nelda, "Do the fairies love the way the goats run and make the bells ring faster?"

"The fairies love any silliness," Nelda said. "They love joy in any form. It makes them want to join in!"

This made me want to skip, so I did. Boris kicked up his heels as we raced down an incline, which made everyone laugh. I had almost forgotten the vultures by the time we rounded the bend …

And then we saw them. Way up at the top of an old snag of fir were a good dozen large, black turkey vultures. I stopped abruptly, and everything was suddenly silent, even the goats' bells.

It was that magical turning from dampness to heat, darkness to light, the pause that comes when a breath is taken in and has not yet begun to leave. Silently, Nelda and I stood with our little herd of goats as twelve pairs of wings were raised and stretched in salutation to the sunlight just burning through. The giant birds sat like kites, wings spread and drying, surreal in their stillness.

No one spoke. Dee and Ester were just coming up behind us. Shafts of sunlight shot through the fog to illuminate patches of redwood sorrel. The vultures' bold red heads bobbed our way. "They see us," I said, finally breaking the silence.

"You bet they do," Nelda replied.

"I think vultures are a Dee kind of bird," I said.

"What are you talking about, Girl?" Dee said, faking annoyance.

"They have a red head, and they like to clean up."

Nelda laughed, but Dee only grunted. Ester had already begun logging, but Nelda and I continued watching until each vulture tucked its wings back and then flapped off for the morning work.

"Sophie, would you pin this up?" Ester had her first list ready:

1 brown paper bag, soggy, "Change for the Hungry", Safeway.

1 two-liter green plastic 7up bottle, 1/8 full.

2 twelve-pack cardboard beer cartons,
   Miller Genuine draft, soggy.

2 crushed hard pack cartons Camel cigarettes, empty.

1 torn sheet lined paper, white.

1 index card holder with blue tab, upper left hand side cut.

1 burgundy oil rag, used.

1 white shoestring, 18 inches.

1 crushed beer can, Coors.

1 white lined paper: "Start 10/24 0000 Stop 11/16 0845 miles Start 11/16 0000"

1 lined white note paper, lipstick stain.

2 post-it note paper, white, each lipstick stained.

1 crushed pack Marlboro, empty.

1 wadded white envelope

1 Styrofoam cup, good condition.

1 lined white notebook paper, scribbled, blue ink.

1 yellow rose bud, wilted.

This pile set Dee off even more than usual. "How dare they!" she seethed. "How dare they! Ride their fat old RV up here, hogging the road, then toss out their trash."

"You don't know it was an RV." Ester pushed herself to a standing position.

"I've got a pretty good idea it was," Dee said as she followed Ester and read over her shoulder. "What else would have eight hundred forty-five miles? An RV from somewhere in Southern California or Arizona."

"And there was a woman who had a yellow rose on their table," I said, "and they checked their oil here and just threw away the oil rag."

"How dare they!" Dee began all over again. She grabbed the sack and began stuffing it with the trash. "I'm not leaving this! It's different with the local rowdies. But now the vacationers!"

Thus began a renewed campaign by Dee to clean up Motorcycle Mountain. Perhaps we can be in touch with what has been dumped for only so long, and then we begin dumping anger ourselves. At least, that's the danger. That day, Dee became even more enraged than usual. The dumping by out-of-town vacationers was harder to take.

We all were mad, to be honest. I'm not sure about Ester, so I shouldn't say she was, but Nelda and Dee and I were, for sure. We had developed a kind of propriety over this Huckleberry fire road. So when Dee started turning the signs 90 degrees to confuse tourists who might be following directions to the top to shoot, or looking for a short cut over the ridge, Nelda and I cheered her on.

It wasn't easy to get the signs to turn. They had been there a long time. So it took three of us, leaning and pushing and grunting until we finally just bent the sign.

"There!" Dee pulled back and looked at our handiwork. The sign looked as if nothing had happened, but it had. And now those individuals looking for the top of the hill would find the bottom, and those seeking a shortcut to the main highway were routed right back to where they started. "People are going to get so lost , they'll wish they never even *thought* of Motorcycle Mountain!" She chuckled to herself.

"It *is* breaking the law," Ester said.

Nelda had been so involved she almost forgot Ester had been there to witness it. "I've never seen a law that says, 'Don't turn road signs ninety degrees.'"

"I'm sure there is such a law," Ester replied. "There're laws about everything else."

"And look where they've got us," Dee answered. "There's laws against dumping, Ester, and as you know, they do absolutely no good, no good at all. Anybody can dump. They can even put their name and address in what they dump, and nothing happens." She wiped her hands on her jeans. "Okay, there's more to do. It will be dark before long."

Nelda chuckled.

"What's so funny?" I asked. Ester had already begun her hillside scanning as we started walking the one-lane road into the dark woods.

"I was just picturing people coming up here to shoot, trying to find the top, and getting to the bottom instead. They'll be far enough down this one-lane road before they figure it out. Then they'll have to circle back on the fire road and try again. They'll end up making an enormous circle, more like worshipers coming to a sacred site than riders intent on shooting up the place."

"They'll be mad as hell," Dee said.

And this made Nelda chuckle again.

TELL ME THE TIME BORIS CHARMED THE DEPUTY.

One day Boris was in rare form. Nelda and I had decided to take the goats to a grove of ancient redwoods at the northern base of Huckleberry Mountain. We left Ester and Dee at the cabin, because it was getting hot and we knew Ester would suffer from the heat. And if we took her with us, and she found garbage, we knew we all would suffer. But the goats needed their browsing time, heat or no heat, so Nelda and I followed the trail around the mountain, stopping occasionally to let the goats browse.

We both had been to the grove before. Everyone in Huckleberry had. Nelda let me lead, and I followed the familiar paths through the oaks and poison oak, through the bay trees and madrones, until the trail descended steeply into the valley of redwoods.

The goats loved poison oak. Not only did they love eating it, but they loved rubbing their heads against the woody stems. We tried to discourage this, because we didn't want to pet them afterwards. When Boris rubbed his head hard in a small clump of it, Nelda exclaimed, "Boris! Now you've done it! No! Get away! No one wants to pet you now!" Boris looked confused but determined to get his head scratched by one of us. He turned toward me and Nelda pushed him away. "Careful, Sophie! Just keep walking." She rubbed mud on Boris' head at the next streambed to absorb the poison oak oil and then rinsed the mud off. Boris really hated this and bucked about. He reared up to butt, and Nelda scolded again. So he got started early that day on his butting game.

I often hiked animal paths barefoot, and that morning I had pulled my shoes off the minute we started. Being barefoot always slowed me down, and the goats appreciated this, because it gave them a lot of time to browse. My feet had ears and listened to the path, but I had to go very slowly to hear. Then I learned of soft decaying redwood needles, of the slight pain of a stick here and there, of the relief of bare earth. When I sat on a rock to brush off the soles of my feet, I chewed a leaf of redwood sorrel, that delicate lacy dancer of the redwood forest, and sourness burst in my mouth. "Nelda, feel this path," I said. "It is *so* soft ..."

"Looks good," Nelda said, sitting down on a log. She started untying her boots and was immediately surrounded by five goats trying to get at the laces. It was the rascally Boris who actually swallowed a lace, and Nelda had to gently pull it out. She rubbed his back, and he arched his neck back and puffed his hair up to more thoroughly enjoy it.

Both barefooted now, we headed into the dappled shade. Now Nelda led. The goats walked single file, behind her and in front of me, grabbing mouthfuls of leaves here and there. They gorged on one plant, ignored another. Hornsby was the last in the walking line, Natalie always the first. Emily and Boris or Tarquin would make sure everyone stayed in the correct order. Even I was butted if I tried to step ahead of anyone, and today Boris was the one to do the butting. Nelda scolded, but it didn't faze him.

We entered the cool darkness of an ancient grove, one of the few untouched by the loggers. Here and there were trees that had naturally fallen, and I walked the trunks like sidewalks, or thick tight wires, the goats close behind me. Almost all the standing trees had blackened bark at their bases from the fires that periodically cleaned the forest floor. Sometimes the fires found their way into the hearts of trees and flamed up within, creating living caves. I entered these caves with their charred walls reverently, like I might enter a temple, sitting in the darkness until my eyes adjusted. The walls had a rippled smoothness to them and stretched up farther than the light could illuminate. There was such peace inside those burned out trees — and mystery, too.

When a huge redwood falls, it lies almost forever on the forest floor, melting into the earth so slowly, leaving behind a ring of descendants, many of them becoming tall, lithe, sturdy trees in their own right. Such redwood rings were scattered all over Huckleberry Mountain. They were common in the areas that had been logged, but they were present in the ancient grove, too.

"Look how the trees grow in circles," I said.

"Witch's circles," Nelda said. "Stand in the center spot. That is where the redwood mother grew."

We walked through the thick mat of needles under the youthful trees and into the indented bowl of the center. "Close your eyes," Nelda said. "Just feel."

The goats were happy to stop and browse a few minutes. I could hear them in the brush nearby as I stood there with my eyes closed. Bells tinkled. I felt Boris' warm, wet mouth nibbling on my fingers. The air smelled somewhat acidic, but rich and comforting. As we stood in the spot where the redwood mother had lived, I felt calm and somehow larger. "Nelda, I feel bigger!"

Nelda laughed. "Trees do that," she said.

"But there's no tree here!" I said.

"Oh, yes, she's still here," Nelda said. "This is the place she grew those many years, making her seeds, and it was the place she fell. She's still here in spirit. That's what you feel!"

And I did. I raised my arms high, up toward where the mother tree used to splay her needles to catch the fog and condense it into rain, creating this forest. I breathed in the tinge of her perfume, which lingered even after all these years. That smell is like no other, a rich and earthy fragrance that hints of secrets held for centuries, for this mother tree must have been many hundreds of years old when she fell. To stand where she grew was to stand in the heart of her. I basked in her presence. If you stood there long enough, listening, I thought, you would surely come to understand many things.

Walking back toward the cabin, we stood in every ring we came across, the ones where the mothers had been cut down by loggers and the ones where the mothers had simply fallen from old age. The other goats browsed, but Boris always went right into the ring with us and then rubbed his head briskly on pieces of stump, on bark, on the bay trees that often sprout up around the redwood circles.

When we were almost home, we came across one of the road signs we hadn't turned, and I suggested to Nelda that we do it for Dee. Which is what we were doing when the deputy came around the corner on foot.

"Ma'am, what are you doing?"

We jumped three feet straight up. "Turning this sign," Nelda said without thinking.

"That is what I've been doing myself," he said. He looked young and innocent. "Someone has been vandalizing them."

"I know," Nelda said.

"Your goats are loose." The deputy was staring in amazement at the eight goats scattered over the hillside and road. Boris was walking toward him, ever ready to investigate something new.

"They are very good goats," I said.

"You know, they have a potential for being a real nuisance to the neighbors."

"Nelda's goats are very well behaved," I insisted.

The deputy pulled a pad of paper out of his hip pocket and a pen from his shirt, which knocked his package of cigarettes to the ground. Now Boris was *really* interested. "I better get your name ..." the deputy began, looking at Nelda.

Just then Boris grabbed the cigarettes and started eating the entire pack.

"Hey, you, give me back my smokes!" the deputy exclaimed, but I could tell he was amused that a spunky goat had gotten his cigarettes. As he leaned down to pull the pack out of Boris' mouth, Tarquin grabbed the pad of paper. "Jesus!" the deputy yelled, grinning. "These are attack goats!"

"Well, they do like paper and tobacco," Nelda conceded. Now the deputy was grabbing for the pad of paper. Boris reared up to butt him and the deputy pushed his head, which only excited Boris more. He had been primed earlier in the day for a good butting, with his head washing and all, and he was ready!

The fat black goat stood on his hind legs, making himself as large as possible, and danced toward the deputy, prepared to deliver a blow. The deputy pushed him again and they played this way for several minutes. Nelda and I kept glancing at each other and tried not to smile too much.

Finally the deputy tired of the game and Nelda rubbed Boris' back to distract him. It took a lot of rubbing. "Great critter," the deputy said. "I've got to get on investigating these vandalism reports, though. My boss wouldn't approve if he thought I was playing butting games with a goat. Let me know if you see anyone suspicious."

"Sure will," said Nelda.

"Sure will," I said.

TELL ME THE TIME THE GOATS CAUSED PANDEMONIUM.

Ever since Ester received the card announcing her niece's impending visit, Dee had been devising a plan to entertain them. We all knew where Ester would end up if we didn't have a good plan. Dee was quite good at figuring such things out, but her plans almost always had a fatal flaw.

Dee's plan for the current problem was this: we would fix up the abandoned house on the last dead-end lane off the Huckleberry fire road enough to entertain the niece and her husband for the afternoon. The paint on the house was still in decent shape—it was a cute little white cottage some family must have once used in summer. No one appeared to have been here for some time, though. We surmised that the couple had died, leaving the cottage in its cared-for state to their children, who hadn't used it but hadn't gotten rid of it, either. It would make just the right spot for entertaining Ester's niece.

We visited the cabin several days in a row to check out the traffic, and there was absolutely none. The cabin was built on stilts on a hillside, with a rickety deck overlooking the river far below. We planned to sweep the deck and path and straighten the small rooms, until the miniature bungalow looked right for a couple of little old ladies.

There were two closet-sized bedrooms in the back, one for Dee and one for Ester. There was also a small living room that would easily seat three people and a kitchenette with sunny French-paned windows overlooking the deck.

One of the risky parts of the plan was getting into the cabin. To break into a house is trespassing, we knew that, but there was no way around it.

"We would ask if we knew who to ask," Dee said.

"I doubt that!" Nelda answered. "You would ask to use someone's abandoned house for the afternoon?"

"Since we don't know who to ask, it doesn't matter, does it?" Dee answered. "Here, help me turn this sign." Dee was in the habit these days of keeping the signs on the mountain spinning. She was highly annoyed that the deputy had time to straighten the signs, but not to follow up on the garbage dumping.

"How will we get in, Dee, if we don't have a key?" I asked.

"Not much of a problem," Dee answered. "There's an unlocked window. I checked that out long ago. "

"She's an expert in these matters," Nelda added.

And she was, too. Dee had learned through decades of practice to move in such a way that she would not be noticed. I guess we all had learned to do that.

Dee knew if we moved with the flow of the neighborhood we would probably not be noticed. Our best bet was to avoid standing out, though later I wondered how any of us imagined we could go unnoticed for long—three vagabond women, a scruffy-looking young girl, and eight goats!

Nelda hoisted me into the back bathroom window, where I climbed onto a small cabinet and then down to the floor. The room smelled of mildew and mouse droppings. I found my way into the kitchen, and with Nelda's pushing a little from the other side, pulled the door open, letting the other three in. The goats alternated between browsing in the brush above the house and dozing on the deck.

Each day we swept just a little, leaving the front walk until the afternoon of the big visit. We cleaned the interior rooms first, airing the old chenille spreads on the beds. While we were doing this Ester, of course, insisted on logging everything, to Dee's consternation.

"Ester, come on," she snapped. "This isn't garbage. This is the house where we are going to entertain your niece and her husband." Having said her piece, she went back to dusting the dishes on the open kitchen shelves.

"One wooden table, painted white, four legs, one slightly shorter," Ester said aloud.

"Ester!" Dee said, louder than she meant to. "Come help! Let's get this dusted! And you can't be doing this when Alice is here. She'll have you locked up!"

Ester looked up, as if hearing Dee for the first time. She had been sitting on a chair by the table with her notebook. She strained getting to her feet.

I remember thinking, *She's very old. I hope she can make it with us.* Ester did help Dee dust the rest of the shelves, but the minute they finished, she returned to her logging. "One monkey wrench, rusted; rags, one foot by two feet, greasy ..."

"Ester, stop!" Dee exploded. "This is not a dump. This is a home! You need to start thinking of it that way."

"Honey, if people have left it behind, I must log it."

Ester was like that, living between worlds, in a way. The thing is, she could rally and dust the dishes or carry on a sensible conversation. But then she would go back to logging and we'd all just look at each other, shaking our heads about Ester's strange compulsion.

I had convinced everyone that I could handle staying with the goats all afternoon in the meadow a few hundred feet higher up the Huckleberry fire road. There would be no place for goats that afternoon. Nelda would play the role of Dee's niece who lived nearby, serving coffee and tea and helping any unforeseen circumstances that might occur.

The house was quite charming in its weathered way by the time we finished our chores. Dee had a way of making a house very comfortable and cozy. I found myself wishing we could all move into this little house. It was larger than Nelda's cabin, and there might be room for me, too. The goats particularly liked the deck and its patches of sun and shade. Boris would stand on his hind legs and peer through the kitchen window onto the counter where Nelda set out our lunch, scanning for an apricot or banana. If he saw something he wanted, he walked in, stood on his hind legs, and took it.

Boris was the only goat this assertive, but once he got a piece of fruit or a paper sack with some kind of food in it, the others would suddenly be quite interested. Then they would all come into the house, standing on their hind legs, butting each other and fighting over who would be next to pull something off the countertop. At which point Dee would appear, grabbing the food back and pushing the goats out the door. Since goats are not as cooperative as dogs, they would push back, and all the while one of them would be stealing something else to eat. I would yell and grab Emily or Natalie, and the melee would continue until Nelda appeared, the recognized human leader of this herd. Then as if by magic, all eight goats would suddenly be outside with the door closed. Ester seldom noticed any of this.

The morning of the niece's visit, Nelda, the goats, and I went down the mountain to the cottage to sweep the main walkway. We didn't want to sweep it too much, in case someone happened by and wondered what on earth was going on, but we wanted to make it look recently used so the niece and husband would not be suspicious. They were to arrive at 2:00, but we all wanted to be at our posts by noon in case they arrived early.

At noon, when Dee and Ester came, Nelda walked the goats and me up the road to the meadow and there we had our lunch. It was the time of day when the goats liked to sleep in the shade, so after Nelda and I ate our cheese sandwiches the goats settled one by one into some dried grass in the shade of a giant madrone and were soon all snoring away.

Nelda and I didn't talk much. We were both anxious about how this afternoon would go. Pretty soon Nelda, too, stretched out in the shade and went to sleep, and I went to the nearby spring to make stick boats to shoot the rapids.

In about twenty minutes, Nelda was up. "Okay, Sophie," she said. "You know what to do. I'll be back when it's over. You sure you'll be alright here alone?"

"Sure," I answered, pressing my bare toes into the tiny rivulet of water. The goats still dozed, although I could see their ears turning like radar. Nelda slipped away quietly, so as not to rouse the goats and have them follow her.

Time passed. After a certain while Emily tried to nurse Natalie, who kicked her away. Then Emily came to see what

I was up to. I scratched her back as she stood motionless. I loved the grassy smell of her coat. I tried to hold her but she leapt away. Goats like to be scratched, and talked to, and walked with, and played with, but they do not want to be held on your lap. When Boris saw Emily getting my attention, he butted her broadside, and she butted him back, so I scratched both of them. This brought Hornsby, wanting to get in on the action. Natalie was more composed, being the head goat. She would sometimes allow me to scratch her back, but she certainly wouldn't fight anyone for it. So she stayed a few feet away, eating some madrone leaves in a shade patch.

We played this way for what seemed like hours. The sun was reaching the afternoon hotness that suggests it's always been that way and is never going to end. I decided to walk the goats a little, and once we started walking, I decided to walk to the hill above the cottage for a peek.

It got slightly cooler as we went back down into the redwood forest. Shafts of light shot through the canopy above us. When we got to a knoll overlooking the cottage, I could see Nelda, Dee, and Ester, and along with them a woman in a blue-flowered dress and a man in white shorts and a red short-sleeved shirt. They were all sitting on the deck outside the kitchen, and on a little table in their midst sat a bowl of apricots and peaches. Their voices wafted up like seductive smoke from a neighbor's barbecue.

I sat behind the trunk of a giant fir. The goats browsed on some nearby Scotch broom as I studied each person on the deck. Ester looked alert and sweet, but the niece and husband looked tense and a little bored. Puffs of cigarette smoke bobbed before the man's face, and I could see Dee trying to avoid its drift by moving a little to one side, and then to the other.

Suddenly, there was a rustle in the brush below us. A couple of boys I recognized from school lay on their bellies watching the group on the deck. They each held rifles made from fir branches, aimed at the group below.

The goats also heard the brush rustle, of course, and stood alert, their little flag tails curled back over their rumps. The hair along the ridges of their backs stood straight up. Had they been about three times as big, they would have looked formidable.

Just then, from below, came a laugh, Nelda's musical laugh, rising through the forest like bird song. Or maybe it sounded to the goats like the clear, melancholic notes of Pan's pipe. Boris' head jerked a little in recognition. Then it came again! A trill kind of laugh, genuine and warm. Boris clearly heard the familiar speaking voice, now rising like a lovely scent, then Natalie recognized Nelda's voice, too, and then Hornsby. Their tails relaxed and they began to move.

It is a moment I still remember with horror. I knew I had made a terrible mistake, and that the consequences were out of my control. I knew what was about to happen, that it would cause us all a lot of grief, but there was absolutely nothing I could do to stop it.

Within moments, an avalanche of goats was pushing down the hill toward the deck. Never mind that there were two crouching boys in their way; the goats ran right over them. The sound of brush crackling and boys hollering filled the air. "Natalie!" I screamed. "Boris!" But the goats had now transferred leadership to Nelda and there was no calling them back. Not knowing what else to do, I ran down the hill behind them.

The five people on the deck stood up hastily, or I should say that four did. Ester continued to sit, probably resisting the urge to pull out her notebook. Nelda called to me —"Sophia!"—but I just kept running behind the herd, helpless and horrified that my lack of judgment had caused such a ruckus. I noticed that the boys, too, had jumped up and were running toward home.

The goats kept right on barreling down the slope, and Boris soon spotted the bowl of apricots and peaches on the table. They reached the deck fast, and all eight goats began butting and squashing the juicy fruits in their mouths. When the husband tried to shoo them away, Boris nibbled the cigarette right out of his fingers.

It's hard to say what happened next. In such times, everything seems to happen at once. Nelda took the rest of the fruit off the table and stuck it inside the kitchen door, and the niece ran in and slammed the door behind her. The husband inadvertently got into a butting game with Boris and Tarquin, during which Boris discovered the pack of cigarettes in his shirt pocket and tore a hole in the shirt to get at it.

Nelda grabbed Hornsby's collar, called Natalie, and calmly explained to the shocked visitor that these goats were hers, and that a neighborhood girl (me) had been caring for them during the afternoon. As she spoke, Nelda motioned for me to follow her and help corral the goats out of there.

On the way up the path to the street, we were met by one of the boys' irate mothers, the two boys trailing behind her.

We had just reached the red sports car the niece and her husband had rented for their visit when the mother yelled at Nelda, "What the hell is going on here?"

"We're just getting the goats back up to their pasture," Nelda said.

"My son was injured by those goats," the mother continued. "They knocked him down and stepped on his eye!"

I shot a quick glance at the sheepish-looking boy. He definitely had a bruised and puffy eye.

"Oh, surely not!" Nelda replied blandly, continuing to herd the goats toward the road.

"The boys said they were charged by a whole herd of goats who ran right over the top of them."

"They were laying on the ground already," I said, "pretending to shoot Ester and Dee with rifles and ..."

"The relatives are visiting today after all these years," Nelda broke in. "Probably seemed odd to your son and his friend to see somebody in the house."

"You need to keep those goats penned up!"

Nelda motioned to me to keep walking. By now the husband appeared around the corner of the house, closely followed by the niece. Seeing them, the mother was suddenly sweet as gooseberry jam. "Nice to see you visiting after all this time!" she called to the couple.

"Been too long," the niece called back, a hint of guilt in her voice. "Much too long. Our busy schedules, I guess. We want to make it sooner next time."

Nelda and I exchanged a look. The mother was calming down. Even her Medusa-like hair seemed to relax some. "Keep those goats under cover!" she called to Nelda.

Nelda waved and called to the couple, "I'm going to walk Sophia and the goats back to the pasture."

"Well, we need to be going soon anyway," the husband called.

So Nelda and I walked on up the road. The goats scampered ahead, grabbing a madrone leaf here, a twig of poison oak there. Nelda put her arm around my shoulder.

"Sorry," I said.

"It worked, but it was really a close call," Nelda answered, hugging me.

"We just thought we'd take a walk, and then those boys were hiding and startled the goats, and then they heard you …"

Nelda stopped me. "Sophia," she said, looking at me straight on with her kind eyes. They were a blue green in this light, the color of the redwood canopy and sky combined. "Sophia," she repeated, "this sort of thing sometimes happens when you have goats."

I smiled and put my hand in hers, understanding something new about of love.

TELL ME THE FIRST TIME YOU HEARD THE GOATSONG.

A day or two after the visit with the niece and her husband, Nelda and I took the goats up the ravine to a pool of water. We sat in the coolness of a circle of redwoods several feet away from the pool and watched the goats suck up large amounts of water. After a time, one by one, they settled down around us. Boris, of course, came over to Nelda, and she scratched up and down his spine. His eyes glazed over as he stood absolutely motionless. Even his chewing stopped.

"Nelda," I asked after some time, "how did you ever come to be living with these goats? Why don't you have a job like Ma and live in town?"

Nelda was silent a few seconds as she kept scratching Boris. "I never could live in town," she said. "It's a long story … too long for today."

"Tell me a short version of it," I pushed.

"Well, I used to think it was about unfairness," she began.

"I know," I said. "Nothing is fair."

Nelda looked at me and continued scratching the goat. "I guess I thought things *should* be fair, and when they weren't, I got angry. I moved away from it all to the cabin on Huckleberry Mountain."

"So are you hiding out?" I asked.

"Retreating. There is a difference between hiding out and retreating. But as it turns out, this is the life I was meant for. The goats, the redwoods, the hills, the earth. What more could you want?"

There was a pause. I could feel the heat of Emily, who had lain down beside me. Her breathing was in little huffs. "How do you make money?" I continued. I thought of all the hours Ma worked, how little time there was for anything else.

"I don't need much," Nelda answered. "And I eat a lot from the land. The land is a great mother! The goats provide milk, and I make cheese, and the goats forage. And as you know, when I need something else, I trade some goat cheese. Trading is a good way to live."

"Ma works all the time," I said. I thought about the time we did spend together. "But I don't think I'd want to see her more often," I added.

Natalie lay down at my feet and cleaned her front hoof. "Why's that?" Nelda asked.

"She's mad a lot," I said. "I don't really think I'd want to be around her more. I might like a mother to be around, but not her."

Nelda just nodded. She was stroking Natalie now, which caused Boris to lunge forward, hoping to butt Natalie broadside. "No!" Nelda said firmly. She reached out to scratch his head and he instantly calmed down. After a few minutes, Nelda lay back into the redwood needles. I lay back, too, staring up into the ring of deep green, lacy treetops framing the blue sky.

"By the time I was living here on the mountain," Nelda continued, "I felt different. It was almost like I had a different name. Or maybe I was growing into my true name."

"What is your true name, Nelda?"

"It isn't quite like a name we say out loud or spell with so many letters," she replied. "A name like that only hints at your true name. So I guess if you were putting it in words, like the Indians do, my name might be She-Who-Was-Turned-Away-and-Thereby-Turned-Within, or She-Who-Has-Great-Sadness-and-Great-Joy, or She-Who-Is-Herself."

"Are you sad, Nelda?"

"Sometimes."

"Were you sadder before?"

"No, but I was angrier. I've finally accepted my sadness. Once I accepted things as they are, something amazing happened. The world got brighter, the colors more intense. I found myself looking more carefully at everything. As time went by, I noticed that everything was shimmering like tiny stars. Then, after more time, I saw that everything's made up of tiny stars. When I see this, I feel joy in my heart."

I *almost* knew what Nelda was talking about, but I had never heard words put to it. Her description of the intensity of color and the shimmering stars reverberated within me in a familiar, if also startling, way. It was as if her words illuminated a place in me that until now had existed in shade.

Suddenly three goats were standing over us, sniffing our faces. Nelda laughed and started rubbing Tarquin, then moved on to much shier Mercury. I petted Caramel, a tiny goat with ginger eyes. Her breath smelled like rumen — stinky grass.

"Do you think that Caramel is made of stars?" I asked.

"Everything is," Nelda answered.

"She doesn't *smell* like stars," I said, rubbing Caramel's neck. Caramel froze in place for the petting.

Nelda laughed and looked off into the treetops. There was a hawk screaming down the ravine. Was it celebrating a catch? Calling a mate? As I watched it circling high above us, wings outstretched, I thought about this link between knowing your true name and seeing the stars that everything is made of. All I could do was ask questions, even though I didn't know what questions to ask. "Do you think that hawk knows its true name?"

"Sounds like it," Nelda answered.

I thought of the deer in the meadow we had surprised that morning, the fawn with fading white spots that bounded to the right, the doe that leaped to the left.

"And deer?" I asked.

"They run like it," Nelda said. "They have the confidence that comes when one knows one's true name."

"I think Emily knows her true name," I said. Emily had jumped across the stream and was dancing in circles on a large flat rock. She kicked her hind legs high in the air as she circled.

"She is certainly full of herself," Nelda agreed. "Look how her body sings 'Goat! Goat! Goat!'"

"She's singing a Goatsong," I laughed.

"The saddest song there is," Nelda said.

"What do you mean, Nelda? Goats are almost always happy."

"Goats are hedonists!" Nelda laughed.

"What's a hedonist?"

"Someone who seeks pleasure."

"Then it seems like a Goatsong should be happy."

"I know. But the truth is, a Goatsong involves a sacrifice. Little goats were often sacrificed during rituals in the old days. They still are in many places. Not our goats, of course."

"Goats were *sacrificed*? What do you mean?"

"The life of a goat was offered to a god in order to honor something higher."

"Higher than a goat?"

"Sophia, sacrifice is a sacred act, but people got mixed up about it. Instead of sacrificing their passions and cravings, or sacrificing their material goods so they might know their true essence, they began to ignore the pure bundle of liveliness in themselves, their own version of Emily's dance of *Goat! Goat! Goat!* They began to think other things were more important."

"Like what?" I asked.

"Power, money, things. Being rational. Thinking too much. And in the process, most of us stopped seeing *the stars*, stopped feeling their warmth, if we ever experienced them in the first place."

"So *that's* why a Goatsong's so sad," I said.

"That's why a Goatsong is tragedy," Nelda answered.

After that, we were both quiet for a long time.

SOPHIA, TELL ME MORE ABOUT WHAT WAS ON THE LISTS.

1 beer can, Coors, aluminum, semi-smashed

~

1 beer bottle, label torn and unreadable, green.

1 plastic freezer bag, Safeway, good condition.

1 16 oz. paper cup, 7-11, good condition.

~

15 2-ft. wide, 6-ft. long strips plywood, painted white on one side.

12 1x3 fir lattice, 4-7 ft. long, worn.

~

l page Press Democrat paper, Page D-3

l brown paper bag, empty, crumpled.

~

l corn dog wrapper, Fircrest Farms, empty.

~

Dee pulled a piece of black plastic from the rubble. "One large plastic bag," she said, "black, holes, but otherwise, good condition ... Ester, this stuff doesn't rot. It tears up, but it doesn't disappear. Look, these tin cans are rusting, the paper has almost made it into the ground, but the plastic is unscathed! It's really not disposable."

"Please, continue." Ester was perched with her notepad and pen on the roadside above Dee.

For a moment Dee paused. "Two rusted number five cans, no label ... but we sure do use it like it's disposable. I used to buy bags just like these for my garbage. Every single one of those bags still exists in a landfill somewhere."

"Two rusted cans, that's where you left off." Ester's pen paused over her pad.

"Okay, okay, you old coot! Four empty envelopes, five by eight, white, unopened, clear window, dirty, soft, rotting."

"Dirty, soft, rotting …" Ester echoed.

"Six cigarettes butts, filters, and ashes …"

"And ashes …"

1 large plastic bag, black, holes, otherwise good condition.

2 rusted #5 cans, no label.

4 empty envelopes, 5x8, white, unopened, clear window, dirty, soft rotting.

6 cigarettes butts, filters, and ashes.

TELL ME THE TIME YOU DANCED
NAKED IN THE MEADOW.

That entire summer was one long hot spell, the hottest on record, plenty hot enough to incubate rumors. We thought that we had made it through that visit with the niece and her husband quite well, and a sense of timelessness set in. This can bring on certain problems, like forgetting that we live in a time and space where people are vindictive.

One particular afternoon, we were at the stream where I first met Nelda. Because it was so hot, we decided to wade. Dee changed into a swimming suit and sat on the bottom of the pool, sinking into the water clear up to her neck. The air was absolutely still except for the popping of Scotch broom pods in the heat of the sun and the lulling sound of the water. The goats had all drunk long and deeply when we first arrived at the stream. Now they settled in the shade to doze through the midday while chewing their cuds.

Occasionally, their heads would droop forward until they caught themselves and began chewing again.

Ester napped in the shade, too, resting her back against a boulder. Nelda rolled up her jeans and sat on the stream's edge, soaking her feet in the water. I launched boats of bark and followed them downstream a hundred feet or so, then brought them back to start over. After a while, Nelda gave us some bread and goat cheese that she had brought, and then she and Dee napped, too, while I continued playing with my bark boats in the stream.

The heat brought the luxury of boredom — the kind of boredom that is good for you. Your mind floats and finds things that it would never come onto if you stayed on the busy track all the time. It has to be a worry-free boredom, however, and to me, the quiet here with these three napping women was that way. I had the freedom to follow my imagination into the work of the water skeeters walking on the quiet surface of the creek, to lie on my back in the water like the skeeters and float, watching the osprey overhead from my watery standpoint. It was, quite simply, heaven on earth.

So it was in this state of mind that I experienced the next set of events. As I was lying with my ears submerged in the water, eyes closed, listening to the magnified gurgling of the water, I heard a commotion. It sounded like a sharp percussion of instruments. I sat up. The boys who had been spying on us that day the niece and her husband were visiting had arrived on the scene with their stupid barking dog, startling the goats and the rest of us, too. The goats lost their heads and ran, and of course the dog took off after them.

The minute I saw this, I took off after the dog, throwing rocks. Dee had been in the bushes peeing, and now I heard her behind me, yelling at the boys and the dog. Nelda firmly called the goats' names, remaining calmer than any of us. Soon she had collared the dog, which made the goats immensely more brave. They had returned to help Nelda out with their horns. I grabbed at goat collars, trying to spare the frightened dog. When I turned to see where the boys were, I saw them staring wide-eyed at something behind me. I involuntarily turned and there stood Dee, stark naked. She had taken off her suit in the bushes to pee, and then, without a second thought, had joined the chase.

"Here's your dog," Nelda said, quietly but sternly. "You need to keep her under control if you are going to let her run free. She could hurt the goats, or deer, or other wildlife."

"Uh-huh," the boys grunted, obviously shaken. But then they began to snicker and turned and ran. When they got farther away, they got braver. "Goat Women! Your goats tried to kill our dog!"

Nelda paid no attention, breathing a sigh of relief. Then she caught sight of Dee and her mouth dropped open.

"They surprised me," Dee shrugged.

Nelda, Ester, and I were all speechless. I think we all knew there would be consequences. This incident wasn't exactly being invisible by fitting into the neighborhood!

But Dee did not miss a beat. Holding her arms to the sky in what was probably at first a gesture of defiance, she began a slow dance. Her flaming hair puffed high on her head. Her body was tanned pretty much all over, so she obviously had been out in the sun naked before; we just had never seen her. She placed one foot, toe first, on the ground in front of her, her back straight and her head high, and then pushed forward to repeat the step with her other foot. Her large breasts drooped and sagged from age, as did a good bit of her skin, but she made no apologies as she moved gracefully through the meadow that afternoon.

As the dance tempo picked up, something else happened. Dee's arms embraced the sky, her face washed with sunlight. Slowly, her anger became joy. I watched until I could stand it no longer, then I pulled off my own blouse and shorts and stood naked beside her, placing my right foot out, toe first, arms reaching high into the azure blue overhead.

There is no word to describe the pulsing of the earth through one's feet. I felt its rhythm as I also felt the tingling of sunlight move through my fingertips and down my arms and body into the earth. Back and forth, these sensations, the flowing of life force on our planet.

How long did I dance? Forever! Once I started, I didn't stop. I didn't want to. The freshness of the air, the heat of the sun on my skin … I felt like the animal that I am.

There was more trouble to come, of course. Those boys left, but they doubled back and continued their spying. The stories in town, about the crazy goat woman and the bag ladies and me, grew way out of proportion.

There were consequences, of course, and we lived with those. Oh, how we lived with those! Still, mostly what I remember about that afternoon in the meadow is Dee and me dancing. I remember the daisy chain that Ester wove for me and Nelda wrapped about my head. I remember Boris and Hornsby standing on their hind legs trying to grab the chain as I moved in slow arcs around the invisible axis connecting the great vault of heaven to the solidity of our earth. I remember Nelda humming. She too danced, although she kept on her jeans and T-shirt.

The sun had sunk low by the time we left. Back at the cabin, I sat beside Ester and she smoothed back my dance-dampened hair. There was never a child better tended than I was that day.

SOPHIA, TELL ME THE STORY OF THE FIRES.

Fall was hot in a different way from how the summer had been. The floods of the winter before had washed away some of the cheapest housing, so Ester and Dee were not the only ones squatting in decrepit, abandoned cabins left on the higher ground of the mountain. And those who still had housing were not inclined to be compassionate. The neighborhood became the raw frontier, with people often taking matters into their own hands. There was a grass roots kind of law enforcement. People must have felt pretty desperate to go to the lengths they did.

One of the favored ways to get rid of undesirables was to burn them out, and that fall there was a lot of burning out going on. On Huckleberry Mountain alone, three houses burned.

The first time was in the middle of a September night. Two squatters had moved into an abandoned house on the road below the path to Nelda's cabin. Used syringes were found in the street around the house, and then one day the next-door neighbor found a power cord plugged into one of his outside sockets. The homeless men were using it to run a coffeepot. The neighbor called the police, but of course the power cord and the men had disappeared by the time they came. The homeless men came back almost before the police car was out of sight.

There were reports of some yelling between the neighbor and the men, and a couple of nights later the neighbor settled the feud once and for all. We woke to the wailing of sirens and to the terrifying glow of flaming torches of redwoods. It's a wonder the whole mountainside didn't burn, including the arsonist's own house, but no one was hurt. The investigation was inconclusive. The paper said that the blaze may have started when a fire was built in a malfunctioning wood stove in the living room of the abandoned cabin, implying that the homeless men caused the fire.

I had spent the night at Nelda's cabin, as it was a weekend and Ma probably wouldn't be home at all. We walked down the mountain at first light to see what had burned. Charred remains of a circle of redwoods stood next to the smoking cavity where the house had stood. The firemen and insurance adjusters were there, hosing down the ashes and poking around for clues.

"I'm so glad those homeless men are gone," Dee said, lowering her voice so the fire marshal wouldn't overhear her. "No more syringes, no more angry confrontations."

"But burned out!" Nelda was appalled. "It's barbaric!"

"No, but maybe not as barbaric as letting the whole neighborhood suffer the drug traffic, risk the syringes." She cupped her hand around her mouth and said in a loud whisper, as if I couldn't hear, "What if our girl here picked up one of those and stuck herself accidentally?"

"But they're getting rid of the undesirables — which, let's face it, Dee, some people would say includes us! We don't have jobs. We live in a shack. What if they burn us out, too, because someone doesn't want a bunch of odd women with goats living near them?"

"We're not druggies! How can you even think of us in the same sentence as druggies?"

"Some people see us that way. I bet he does." Nelda gestured toward a balding man with a stomach melting over his belt. He was making notes on a clipboard. "He'd call you and Ester bag ladies. Undesirables. After all, you and Ester were burned out."

Dee glanced over at the insurance adjuster. She imagined him to have a wife at home who spent the day polishing floors and cooking chicken fried steak for her growing family in the evening hours. She herself had once longed to be the keeper of such a household. But Nelda was right. This man would not want her living in an abandoned garage on his road. Yes, he might just think of *her* as an undesirable.

The second house also burned in the early morning hours. We never heard what happened, but again there were rumors about the homeless and drug traffic. When I got to Nelda's cabin the next afternoon, Nelda and Dee were arguing. In the middle of the room sat a forlorn-looking coffee table that had not been there before.

"But why, Nelda?" Dee's voice was almost pleading. "We're clean as we can be. We don't steal anything except what is thrown in the garbage. That's hardly stealing. So what if I collect a few aluminum cans for extra cash?"

"There are rumors, that's all," Nelda said quietly. She sounded worried. "We don't want to do anything more to feed the rumors."

"If I rescue a table from the garbage that was meant for the dump, that makes me an undesirable? What has this world come to?"

"It's not just your rescuing the table from the dump. It's also dancing nude in the meadow. It's the afternoon several funny old women and a bunch of goats stormed some little boys!" Nelda paused, collecting herself.

Dee leaned back in the chair by the tin wood stove. She seemed tired. I looked around at the first place I had ever really felt at home, with its simple but charming, albeit recycled, furnishings. There was only what we needed. A shelf above the sink held four bowls and four plates, each with its unique, untold history. The rug on the floor was faded and stained, but it was still plush in places and soft to sit on.

"We're not homeless," I said. "Look. Nelda has this wonderful cabin. It is warm. Natalie gives us milk. We have each other. What more could we want?"

I remember the look in Nelda's eye just then, and Dee's, too. It was a peaceful look, full of love. Nelda spoke first. "Sophia, you are absolutely right. We are very much at home here. We have a lot. But if we're too different from everyone else, we may well be judged another way."

Dee was quiet a long time after this. We all were. Finally she said, "I won't go through anyone's garbage again." Nelda breathed an audible sigh of relief.

The third burning was the most frightening. We were returning up the mountain late one afternoon and happened to be near the site of the old cottage where we had entertained the niece. There was an acrid smell of smoke in the air, which made the goats nervous, so there was a lot of butting. Nelda talked to them softly and firmly as we followed our noses.

When we rounded a bend in the path above the old place, everyone came to a sudden halt. Even the goats stood motionless. Below was a burned-out hole where the cottage had stood. Only charred remains were left.

"What happened?" Dee said finally. Ester began to walk toward the site, pulling the small notebook from her pocket. Nelda gently grabbed her arm.

"Ester, let's not go down there," she said.

"When did this burn down?" I asked.

"Must have been last night," Nelda said quietly. "But long enough ago that the firemen felt okay about leaving."

"When is this burning out going to end!" cried Dee, outraged.

A girl a couple of years older than me rode up on her bicycle and stopped. Boris immediately greeted her and she rubbed his head while he rubbed right back. "Cute goats," she said.

"Another house burned." Dee's voice was strong, yet invited comment.

"Early this morning," the girl offered. "My dad is a volunteer fireman. He got the call about four AM."

"What happened?" Dee pushed.

"They don't know exactly," the girl said in her singsong way. I could tell she enjoyed passing news on. "They say it may have been started by some homeless women who were living here on and off through the fall."

"Jesus." Dee said. The rest of us said nothing. It was as if the world had been drained of words.

The girl stayed around for a few more minutes. Nelda gently grabbed Ester's arm each time Ester started to walk toward the site. Finally the girl rode on off.

"Were those homeless women us, Nelda?" I asked when the girl was out of earshot.

"We'll never know. We certainly were seen here. We couldn't have been missed," she chuckled, scratching Boris' coat.

"We stuck out almost too much for rumors," Dee said. "We had a very good story for that boy's mother."

"Well, we had obviously cleaned the place up, too. It no longer looked abandoned, although no one was living here. That alone may have been enough to rouse the neighbors' suspicions. After all, they don't want undesirables in the neighborhood."

"Who has the authority to decide who's undesirable?" Dee exploded.

"Maybe we all think we're the desirable ones and anyone very different is undesirable," I said.

Nelda guided Ester up the road on our way back to the cabin. The goats had relaxed and were dancing about like elves. "I think you're on to something, Sophia. And some of us have money and power to back us up," Nelda said. "You and I, Dee, do not."

"But that doesn't make us undesirables!" Dee said.

"Not to us," Nelda answered. "But maybe to them it does. Money and rightness have a way of fusing themselves together, in men's heads anyway."

"What about the men's wives? What do the wives believe?" Dee continued.

"I don't think their wives want to think about it most of the time. Without their husbands, they could be in our shoes. And some of them will be, one day."

"Like Ester," Dee said.

"Like you," Nelda added.

"I was young when he left." There was sadness and resignation in Dee's voice.

Nelda glanced toward Dee. "And you got stuck, alone with a kid to raise, on minimum wage. What did your husband do, anyway?"

"He was a lawyer. Spawned another family, three girls. Never paid a cent of child support to Jonathan. Later on, when he managed to prove to a judge that I was an unfit mother, he got Jonathan, too."

"My husband left when the babies died," Ester said.

This jolted me. "I didn't know you had babies, Ester."

But Ester said nothing more. She just kept walking up the mountain with Nelda beside her to encourage her along should she slow a little to look for garbage. The goats charged ahead, tucking their heads low and kicking their hind legs high.

None of us wanted to get stuck out after dark.

TELL ME THE TIME THAT ESTER'S LOGGING CAUGHT UP WITH HER.

The rains started a day or two at a time in late October, rinsing the forest clean. The morning after, the world was freshened, and cooler than it had been since the spring. The dust settled.

Ester's garbage dumps were washed by these downpours. Once when we came across a dump recently rinsed by a heavy rain, Nelda commented, "Ah! The papers are merging into the ground."

"Or being washed down the mountain!" Dee grumbled. "Off to where they came from. All except these Styrofoam cups." She reached down to pick up a clean white cup, then found three more cups and a bleach bottle.

"That bleach bottle is pristine white," Nelda exclaimed. "It's beautiful! The rain has soaked off its label and dirt. Now it's like a pearl in this garbage heap."

"You're beginning to sound like Ester," Dee grumbled again. Nelda just smiled.

"Maybe life would be different if we gave everything a good look," I said.

"You too, Sophie! Now *you're* sounding like Ester, " Dee exclaimed. Ester just continued her logging, quietly writing everything down.

"We'd be swamped in bleach bottles if we really gave them a look," Dee mumbled stubbornly. She sat a bit away from the garbage pile, up higher and nearer the road. She did not even seem to mind Ester's foraging.

"We could put them in the back of our cabinets to lighten the darker spots," I suggested.

"Too messy," Dee remarked. "And we don't need bleach anyway. It makes clothing white and kills bacteria, but it doesn't know when to stop. It just keeps killing wherever it goes, down the drains of our houses, into the sewers, into the rivers. Even its bottles are around forever. What a price to pay for cleanliness."

Ester spoke, very unlike her when she was so busy logging. "Casting these away has only brought out their true nature." She handed me the paper she had been logging the garbage on:

one pure white plastic jug,

smooth and perfectly formed

two eight ounce cups, Styrofoam,

white, perfect condition

"I'm not going to log this crap for the rest of my days," Dee suddenly fumed. "This cup is from the store in town. I'm going to return it. If they are thoughtless enough to send out indestructible packaging, they need to know where it ends up. Let them do a little of this looking-to-see-what-is-here business."

"They aren't going to do anything with it," Nelda said softly.

Dee's voice raised. "I'll tell them, *Well you had better do something! You sold a drink in this cup and it ended up in a ditch on Huckleberry Mountain. Don't tell me you had nothing to do with it. If you are going to sell food, fine, but at least put it in containers that rot.*"

But Dee didn't return the cup. Maybe Ester was rubbing off on her, too.

The sun was setting earlier and earlier, and we were losing minutes of light each day. The weekend the time changed, we lost a whole hour, which turned out to be disastrous.

Dee and Ester had come to town to get the mail and to meet me after school. I had started staying at the cabin until after supper, and then Nelda walked me down the mountain to Ma's. Because Ma was never home, she didn't miss me. I think she knew I was spending time somewhere else, but we never talked about it.

Anyway, I met Dee and Ester at the senior center at the edge of town and the three of us started our climb up the mountain. Evening was coming on quickly. The sky began to thicken with dark clouds and we could tell it was going to rain soon.

The first part of the path up the mountain was an asphalt road, and we covered that quickly, especially since no one ever dumped garbage there. But as we made the turn to the fire road and the wilder parts of the mountain, there was a pile of fresh garbage. Dee involuntarily groaned.

By now the clouds were low and the color of trouble. Ester's gait slowed.

"We can't, Ester, it's getting dark and it's going to rain," Dee said.

But Ester did not seem to hear. She stopped and began her poking. "Sophie, write this down, honey," she said.

"Don't you dare, Girl!" Dee said. "Ester, we aren't logging this evening. It's too late."

But Ester went right on. It did not matter how much Dee objected.

Dee wrapped her gray sweater around herself — it was getting cold — and said, "You are more nutty than any of us thought!" Of course, this didn't bother Ester. She kept right on.

I didn't know what to do. On the one hand, Dee was right. It was going to get dark before we knew it, and it was going to rain. On the other hand, there was no deterring Ester. Best to just pitch in and get the job done, I figured, so I started logging.

Finally Dee joined us, whirling through the pile like an eggbeater. I wrote quickly to keep up with them both.

"Twenty-four shotgun shells," Ester called to me.

Dee mumbled under her breath, "Probably another deputy. They have time for target practice, but they don't have time to follow up on who the hell is dumping all this garbage! Maybe they're doing it themselves!"

"Two lotto tickets, scratched," Ester continued.

"Ever hopeful," Dee quipped.

"Six packets of mustard, unopened."

"Why do they hand out so many? Such a waste!"

"Two packets mustard, squeezed and empty."

"And that is plenty, too!"

"One empty matchbook cover, 'Landon White Bail Bonds.'"

Dee was silent.

"What are bail bonds, Dee?" I asked.

"Money you put up to get out of jail before a trial, money that is a promise you'll return for the trial."

"What if you don't keep your promise?"

"You lose the money," Dee said, shrugging. "This sucker's been in trouble," she added.

"What do you mean," I asked.

"Nobody goes to a bail bonds place except someone who is in trouble with the law. Or has a friend who is in trouble."

"How is he in trouble with the law?" I persisted.

"How would I know?" Dee said, still impatient.

"One black ballpoint pen with a blue cap," Ester continued. "One sheet Christmas card stickers, 'Happy Holidays and a heartfelt thanks from your friends at Paralyzed Veterans of America.'"

"Is he paralyzed?" I persisted.

"How can we know these things?" Dee sounded exasperated. "Maybe he just gave some money to the Paralyzed Veterans of America."

"He's in trouble with the law, and he's giving money to Paralyzed Veterans of America?" I said.

"Well, at least they're hoping for a donation from him," Dee said. "Meanwhile he dumps his garbage here."

"I hope he's not paralyzed," I said. "If I was paralyzed and in trouble with the law, I might dump garbage, too."

"I sure hope you wouldn't!" Dee said loudly, but her voice was not so agitated.

"Here, Sophie," Ester called, "give me a hand up." I tacked her list to the tree above the pile:

24 shot gun shells.

2 lotto tickets, scratched.

6 packets mustard, unopened.

2 packets mustard, squeezed and empty.

1 empty matchbook cover, "Landon White Bail Bonds."

1 Black ballpoint pen with blue cap.

1 sheet Christmas card stickers, "Happy Holidays and a Heartfelt thanks from your friends at Paralyzed Veterans of America."

A large plop of rain hit my hand as I tacked up the list, then another. And then the sky simply turned wrong-side out. The sudden darkness was not just from the onset of evening; it was from the massive amounts of water inside the clouds.

I tried to help Ester get back up on the road, but the hillside was quickly liquefying and she slipped onto her knees. Dee quickly appeared by my side. We grabbed both of Ester's hands and pulled her up with us.

I had on a jacket, but a jacket is nothing when you're dealing with the quantity of water that was falling to the earth that evening. Dee and Ester both wore plastic ponchos, so they both stayed somewhat dry — but only somewhat. We were being pounded with rain, and after two minutes, staying dry was no longer the issue. The issue was getting to the cabin safe and sound.

Streams formed very quickly along the edge of the road, and soon they became rapids. The rushing was a song the water was singing to me, to Ester, to Dee. *This way!* it sang, *This way! Up! Follow me up!* I told Dee the water was singing, but I couldn't tell if she answered. The storm was that loud, and she was busy walking with Ester.

As the darkness took over completely, the stream's song became more important. We could no longer see the road. There was only the rushing song to our right to guide us. The redwood and fir whipped in the winds, and the rain stung my face. Dee's flashlight was so dim that we used it for only the most difficult of spots.

In the excitement of the storm, it did not occur to me that it could cause big problems. I felt at one with the wildness of the wind, listening to the big secrets being told among the treetops. The rapidly growing stream in the ditch continued to sing, *This way, this way up!*

So it was not until we reached a very dark area, and Dee stopped and turned on the flashlight, and it faded to nothing, that I realized how serious our trouble was.

"I can't see a thing," Dee said. "It's pitch black. How are we going to get back?"

"We are going to do our best," Ester said.

"We're going to do our best," Dee mimicked. Then she mumbled to me, "At least we don't have to worry about long stops for garbage—unless we find something that glows in the dark. Oh, please, don't let us find anything that glows in the dark!"

"That would mean it was radioactive," I added.

"We definitely do not want to find radioactive garbage," Dee said.

We had no choice but to stand there in the absolute darkness until the rain let up. There was not a hint of light from anywhere. "We can't go anywhere if we can't see the edge of the road," Dee continued. "It's too easy to slip off the edge." So we huddled together for warmth and just waited.

It's strange what you think of at such times. That night, I suddenly thought of the stars that Nelda told me everything is made of. If only they would light up now! But then I remembered how the trail could speak to my bare feet and I got an idea.

"Just hold my hand, Dee!" I said, taking off my shoes, which were soaked anyway. The ground felt cold and slippery. I walked slowly, being careful not to get into the grassy area along one side or into the leaves on the other. The wind blew hard again, shaking the trees, precipitating another momentary shower.

We inched along, seeing absolutely nothing but listening with every cell of our bodies: to the stream, to the wind, to the trees. I didn't *see* the stars, but I felt the guidance of the stars in the hard-packed, slippery earth through the soles of my feet, and heard the stars in the rushing, gurgling water in the ditch. As we neared the top of the mountain, the stream's song grew quieter, and the night air chilled us to the bone. "I hope Nelda has a fire going when we get back," Ester said.

"I bet she's worried," I said.

"I'm sure she would never suspect that we are stupid enough to be out here without even a decent flashlight," Dee said.

We were quiet again. I continued to let my feet be guided by the road. The stones poked hard, so I walked as lightly as I could. Then, after what seemed like an eternity, I saw a small light bobbing in the distance. "Dee," I shouted, "someone else is out here, too."

We had taken the wrong trail, it turned out. Nelda had been looking for us from the minute it started raining. I remember Nelda's light growing nearer. I remember wrapping my arms around her waist, the wetness of her poncho against my cheek. My feet were stiff with the cold. "Sophie, where are your shoes!" she said. And I told her about feeling and hearing the stars in everything, how the road was helping my feet find our way. How I'd heard the stream's song. About the storm's secrets in the treetops, and how the darkness had made it so important for me to hear all of this. "Honey, you'll freeze," was all she said as she helped me put my shoes back on. "Come on, I need to get you all home."

Ester was very weak when we got to the cabin, and it soon became clear that she was ill. She stayed in for two weeks, Nelda nursing her with herbs and her other special remedies. We all worried. The cabin was a long way from town and a medical doctor, and there was no way to get Ester there anyway in her current condition. But as the winds continued to whip the trees day after day, the woodstove warmed the cabin and Ester got better.

Ester never seemed worried about her own health. She liked being inside and slept a lot. Dee grumbled some about how Ester's logging had almost given us all pneumonia. I reminded her how the forest and the stream had helped us back, maybe in exchange for all the attention Ester was giving to the garbage. I said I thought the forest liked Ester and would help get her well. Dee just grumbled some more.

SOPHIA, TELL ME THE TIME ESTER
FOUND THE DEAD BABY.

Ester's strength was slow to recover. She couldn't join us on our rounds for a couple of months, and then she began to take short walks to the meadow nearby in the middle of the day, when the sun was warm and the winds were not telling stories in the treetops.

One unseasonably warm day in late February, Nelda suggested we all go to a meadow on the other side of Huckleberry Mountain. She said Ester was well enough and would benefit from a longer walk.

The way we crossed the mountain was basically an animal path that had been used some by humans, so it had gotten worn and free of heavier brush. We were familiar with the area to the right of the orange trumpet bush where deer bedded. That's where the trail curled around the California sage bush before disappearing again into the density of the oak and bay forest. Nelda and I waited with the goats for Ester and Dee to catch up. As Dee reached us, she swore, "Damn it, Nelda, I'm an old woman! Ester's an old woman! We can't do this!"

"You just did," Nelda answered.

"And one of us might have a heart attack, too! Ester's been sick! Have you forgotten?"

"This is strengthening if you do it slowly."

"Oh, hogwash!" Dee was tired of Nelda's comments that disregarded what she considered common sense. "Girl, what are we doing out here with two crazy women?"

I didn't answer, of course. This was just the way Dee liked to talk. I let my eyes wander back down the mountain to see how Ester was progressing and saw her, standing still as a deer. "Ester's stopped," I said involuntarily. "And she is way off the trail."

Dee sighed. "She's found some garbage, no doubt."

Nelda frowned, making an intense crease between her eyes. Then the crease melted, and she took a deep breath and let it out. "Let's help her."

"We ought to help her, alright," Dee muttered under her breath. "Right to the loony bin!"

The three of us started reluctantly back down the trail. Even the goats didn't want to turn around, Natalie calling to us for several minutes before deciding she would lead the herd back down the mountain.

I remember watching Ester as we walked down the trail. It was one of those afternoons when the grass is so green you think its stars will burst into flame. Against this backdrop, Ester could have been a watercolor, vividly pastel. She wore a blue calico dress that Dee had found in the senior free box. The skirt came almost to the ground, and there were tiny orange poppies around the hem. In her frozen pose she seemed different somehow, more delicate than usual, but oddly more present, too, like a light had just turned on inside her and was coming out through her skin.

Dee continued mumbling under her breath. "I thought we were safe, or I'd never come this way. This is an animal trail! Animals don't litter. Dammit, I've got ticks all over me! Every time I walk on these trails, I get ticks."

Nelda and I were almost to Ester when the stench reached us. There in the trees, beneath some bushes, was a small bundle. As we neared it, Nelda gasped, "The stench! What on earth … ?"

"Newborn," Ester said, and the sound of her voice caused Nelda to rush toward her. Tears were running down Ester's cheeks. "Wrapped in a gray terry towel. Rotted and partly eaten." She was jotting down notes on the pad of paper she held.

"My god," Nelda said. "My god."

That was all there was to be said. I felt dizzy and took hold of Nelda's hand. The goats did not come anywhere near. We heard shuffling as Dee plowed through the dead leaves behind us. "What stinks?" She stopped short. "That looks like …"

"It is."

"Who would have …"

"My god," Dee said, as if repeating after Nelda.

A tortured silence fell, and the stench rose up about us like smoke. Ester wept. We all stood there a long time, still as the oaks about us. I don't know where the goats were. There was no birdsong, only the roar of the insides of the earth.

Finally, Ester broke the spell by wiping her cheek on her sleeve, tearing the top piece of paper from her pad, and handing it toward me. "Honey, would you tack this to the tree there beside you?" Her voice broke, but she pulled herself together quickly. I took the paper and pulled a tack from a tin I kept in my pocket for the purpose. I pushed the tack through the paper and into the soft bark of a black oak.

Newborn

wrapped in gray terry towel

rotted and partly eaten

"We can't just leave it," Dee said. "We've got to call the police."

"Why?" Nelda said, simply.

"We can't leave a dead baby with a piece of notepaper above it, pinned to a tree, just like we do the garbage piles."

"Calling the police isn't going to help the baby," Nelda said quietly. "But I guess we could bury it." Ester had already turned and was shuffling her way through the leaves to the trail.

"But what about who did this?" Dee continued. "We can't just bury the evidence!"

"Calling the police would only get some poor girl in trouble, if they found her at all," Nelda said. She grabbed a stick and started digging through the leaf mold to the loose soil. "Sophia, you go catch up with Ester."

Dee watched Nelda a moment in disbelief, and then got a stick herself. I left without a word, and neither of them said anything else, at least as long as I could hear.

It's strange what you remember of such shocking events. Like the path, how fresh it was from the rain of the last couple of days, the dry brownness of the past season's grass flattened. I remember how the sun was lemon color, how the black oaks had miniature reddish leaves just budding out. And I remember Ester, moving steadily up the path, the border of orange poppies waving about her ankles and calves with every step. I remember the huffing percussion of her breath, like the *whoosh! whoosh!* of a large turkey vulture flying overhead. And when I finally caught up with her, I remember the dampness of her cheeks, like a dam had finally overflowed, and now the lowlands were being flooded.

Most of all, I remember that as we walked, the goats came, leaping about, and when we reached the crest of the mountain and started down the other side, they gambled sideways, kicking their heels high and dropping their heads low.

We had gone a surprising distance when Nelda and Dee caught up with us. "Wait up!" Dee called. "I need a rest." Ester stopped in her tracks but did not turn around. We waited a few minutes, saying nothing, as Dee breathed slower. Finally Nelda said, "Let's stop for a while at the top of this trail. Then we can sit down." Ester started walking, and we followed.

There was a fallen log at the top, and Ester eased herself down onto it. Dee sat beside her, as Nelda and I sank into the grass. A mockingbird sang crazily.

"We buried it," Dee said finally.

Again, no one spoke.

"I mean, we had to! We can't just leave that little body out here to the elements! And I guess we can't report it either. Won't do that baby no good to report it anyway. Too late for that baby. Only get some poor girl in trouble."

A bee buzzed as Dee continued. "Won't help the baby, that's for sure. The baby's dead. What we do or don't do won't make a difference there."

Nelda chewed on a piece of grass. "No one's arguing with you," she said quietly.

"She is!" Dee said, pointing to Ester.

Ester looked up.

"You are too arguing with me. You aren't saying a damn thing, but we all know what you're thinking. You're thinking we were wrong to bury it."

"It doesn't really matter very much to me what you did," Ester said.

"Jesus." Dee kicked the dirt, then turned to Ester. "A damned baby is abandoned, dies, is half eaten by a coyote, and it doesn't interest you what happens?"

"I found one in a garbage bin once," Ester said. "The umbilical cord was still attached, and there was the awfulest mess of blood."

We all looked at Ester, shocked. Her eyes were filled with tears, her hands neatly folded in her lap. She looked like one of those first spring wildflowers—a shooting star, perhaps—heart shaped, blooming when winter storms are still beating the life out of the grasses and trees. Yet this delicate form, there on its slender stem, still expresses its violet pink.

Finally Nelda stood up, gently extending a hand to Ester. "It's getting late, we need to go." Ester's eyes met hers for a second. Nelda smiled. "If I am going to be responsible for you, I've got to get you going."

"You don't have to be responsible for *me!*" Dee snapped.

"Okay." Nelda started up the trail, and I slipped my hand into hers. Ester and Dee followed, and we made our way back to the cabin.

By the time we got there, the silhouettes of redwoods were fading into the darkness. The goats, nervous to be out so late, were quick to go into their pen. I fed them as Nelda grabbed several logs and some kindling on her way through the door. Dee opened two cans of ravioli to heat on the top of the woodstove once it heated up.

Ester sunk into the rocker, visibly exhausted. She slowly began rocking, back and forth, the chair creaking loudly to announce each round. Nelda wadded newspaper and stuffed it into the deep tin stove, then piled on dried oak twigs and lit the fire. She sang until the flames were burning strong. "Rise up, oh Flame!" she sang, over and over. The words leaped from her throat, and the flames seemed to obey her command.

Except for Nelda's singing, it was quiet — and except for the *creak, creak! creak, creak!* of the rocker and the crackling of the flames as they licked the kindling.

"Didn't know you sang," Dee said after a while.

Nelda eyed her, checking for sarcasm, but Dee's face was surprisingly soft. "I don't usually," Nelda said, adding a larger log.

Creak, creak. Creak, creak.

"I used to rock my babies. I had an old rocker, kind of like this one, and I kept it in the kitchen," Ester said.

Creak, creak. Creak, creak.

She continued. "Babies need rocking. It reminds them of being inside their mamas."

Creak, creak. Creak, creak.

"Funny thing is, I don't remember how many there were any more," Ester said. "The first was a boy. He lived a week. The girl lived a day. Some of them never even got to be born properly. They just slipped away before they had even gotten to take their first breath. Don't even know what happened to their bodies."

Creak, creak. Tears again. "I wanted their bodies, but they wouldn't give them to me. Said they were only tissue, that their spirits were somewhere else. Except for the boy and girl. We buried them in the woods in the little cemetery behind the church where my mama and daddy were married. No one came, of course. People just want you to get over it. Get on with it, have another. Replace it. Those first two I wrapped in flannel, and I rocked them one last time before we put them to rest. I rocked them and I sang. The others I never got to sing to. I asked for their bodies, but the doctor said, there are no bodies …"

Creak, creak. Creak, creak.

As we sat there in the firelight, I wished Ma wanted me as much as Ester had wanted her babies. Perhaps all of us were wishing that for ourselves just then. But Dee broke the wishing. "I don't understand how a mother could have left her baby in the woods."

"Maybe she was just scared," Nelda said quietly. "Maybe she was young and never told anyone she was pregnant."

"Did she think the wolves were going to raise it?" Dee's voice gained volume. "Wolves or bears?"

"What makes you think she thought at all?" Nelda said. "She may have been too scared to think. Maybe she just wanted to forget. She wasn't ready to know what she'd done, so she hid it."

"No, she killed it!" Dee said emphatically. "She left it to die slowly of exposure and hunger, or be killed by an animal."

"Partially eaten," Ester said. "Wrapped in a gray terry towel."

"You don't have to tell me," Dee said. "I saw it. I'm not the one to keep telling." The stove was pulsing with heat now, and she poured the ravioli into an aluminum pan she'd found in the garbage behind the deli. "Maybe the boyfriend got rid of it. It was born in some car, and he took it away and hid it."

"Maybe it was born dead," Nelda ventured.

The women fell quiet. Dee put the pan on the stove and it started to sizzle immediately. No one spoke as Dee stirred the ravioli with a silver spoon she'd saved through the years. "That babe didn't have a chance! Not a speck of a chance!" she sputtered. "But then, maybe it's better that way. Look at me. What would I have missed if my mother had left me in the woods?"

"Well, for one thing, the four of us wouldn't be sitting here now," Nelda quickly pointed out. "You'd never have shooed Ester up this hill. She'd be cooling her heels in a nursing home somewhere so medicated she wouldn't know where she was, if not for you being here."

Dee's eyes met Nelda's. For a moment I thought she looked grateful. But she instantly shifted the conversation with, "Supper's ready. Give me your plates."

Ester got up unsteadily, walked to the crate under the window, and lifted out four wooden bowls and spoons. Dee carefully dished out the ravioli, putting seven into each dish. "There're a few left," she said, "if anyone wants them." Which we all knew usually meant me.

Each of us settled into our own spot with a bowl. My spot was on a box under the window that looked out on the goat pen. The fire flared around the log Nelda had added earlier. We ate in silence. Occasionally Ester leaned back — *creak!* — and rested. As the fire died down, the room darkened. Outside, a million stars became visible in the night sky, and we knew that storm was over.

14

SOPHIA, TELL ME THE TIME
ESTER LOGGED DEE.

Although Ester continued her logging, she wasn't quite as intent on it after she found the baby. She laughed more often and talked more, too. But it seemed no matter how many lists we tacked up, people still came and dumped. And houses still burned. Nelda was worried. She said we were living in such an unconventional way that we were sure to catch attention.

One evening after I intercepted a note from the school to Ma about my absenteeism over the last months, Nelda, Dee, Ester, and I sat in front of the fire, warmed by each other's presence. That evening we were each in private worlds of concerns. "What if Ma finds out I'm never at home?" I asked Nelda. "What if she finds out I cut school?"

"I don't know, Sophia," Nelda said quietly, "but I think you have to worry more about the authorities than your mother." She paused. "Besides you *should* be in school."

"I'd rather be here on the mountain."

"It's your job to go to school. And you will attract attention if you don't go. It's one of those times you need to move with the flow, go to school, if you don't want to be singled out."

"But I'm singled out if I go," I said. "All the others have mothers and dads and brothers and sisters. They go visit each other after school. I'm tired of being different and no one playing with me."

"Well, play with *them*, dammit! Play with them!" Dee exploded. "Girl, don't *let yourself* stand out."

Nelda cast a glance at Dee. I said nothing. Dee was prone to exploding when she was worried and upset, and there was nothing to do about it.

"Okay," Dee conceded to the silence. "I know it's not that easy. But you are going to get picked up by the county, Sophia, if you don't find a way to go to school and not stand out."

This made me very sad. Just sitting by the fire with these three women brought the greatest pleasure I had ever known. They cared about me. "How can I feel so happy sitting here and be so worried all at once?" I said.

"Sometimes it's easier to feel life when things are going bad than it is when they are going well. When things are going well, we tend to not pay much attention," Nelda said.

"You mean, it's better if things are going bad, Nelda? It's better because then we are more alive?"

"Not quite what I mean," she said. "When things are going bad, it is tempting to blame ourselves or someone else for the badness, and lose sight of an excellent opportunity."

"What opportunity?"

"If you can *stay awake* when things are bad as well as when they are good, you will see there is a common element in both. A common *juice*."

"Nelda, you're teaching that girl nonsense! Utter nonsense! How is she ever going to make it in this world if you go about telling her stuff that makes absolutely no sense and acting like it's important?" Dee was sitting in the corner of the room, and she had just about had it with all this talk of juices and goodnesses and badnesses.

"But Dee, aren't you more likely to be open, prayerful even, when you're upset in some way? Aren't you more likely to be on your knees?"

"Don't talk to me about being on my knees!" Dee bellowed. "I've spent a hell of a lot more time on my knees washing floors than you've ever spent, and believe you me, it hasn't felt like praying."

"Rocking is praying," Ester chimed in, from her rocker. "Rocking back and forth, back and forth, that is praying. Looking in garbage heaps is praying."

Dee snorted and got up, walking to the counter. "These are crazy women," she said to me. "Believe you me, these two women here are crazy. Do not even try to understand what they are saying because what they are saying does not make sense."

"But I think it might make sense." I said. "I think it might make more sense than thinking we will go to heaven if we do everything right."

Nelda turned as I said this. "You got it, kiddo. It's so simple, so obvious, but we lose track of it when we try to live the life we *think* we should have. The real juice comes from an open attitude toward life and people, plants and the earth, not from doing things in somebody else's right way. It's an attitude like prayer, when we are most open to the star nature of everything. And sometimes that attitude is easier to hold when things are not on the course we're satisfied with, when we get derailed."

"Jesus!" Dee said. And that was the end of the discussion.

But it gave me another way to look at what was soon to come, as well as the courage to bear it. These women were my teachers. I learned so much in the short time I spent with them, and one of the biggest lessons was what to do with anger.

We had finished logging a particularly large fresh heap of garbage one afternoon. I'd gone to school that day, as I had done recently, making sure to act like the others. I volunteered for the baseball games, and I even volunteered to help the teacher at noon hour. When she asked nosy questions, I gave her normal replies. *Yes, I had had breakfast that morning. Yes, my mother had heard about open house. No, she didn't come because she had to work that night.* I created a girl named Sophia to stand in my place for me, and I let the teacher get to know that girl.

I was pinning up a logging list with a thumb tack when Dee exploded. "I am so tired of this! They will never stop dumping."

"And you will not stop caring that they dump, either," Nelda said wryly.

"But what does it matter if I care or not?" Dee was exasperated.

Ester reached into her pocket and pulled out the notebook. We each held our breaths, hoping that she had not spied another pile, as it was getting late. But instead she walked toward Dee until she was about two feet away and then scribbled on the pad. She tore the sheet off and handed it to me. "Sophie, honey, find a place to put this on Dee."

I stepped forward and took the slip of newsprint with the scribbled pencil writing. I read it slowly to myself and involuntarily looked up into Ester's eyes. They were smiling, although her face was absolutely serious. I read it aloud:

One old woman,

short and plump,

flaming hair.

Nelda burst out laughing. After a pause, Dee did too, and Ester's face relaxed into even more of a smile.

"Anyone have a safety pin?" Dee asked.

"I have one here somewhere," Nelda said, rummaging through her pack.

I pinned the note to Dee's shirt just over her heart. "Yes!" Dee laughed. "This needs to be seen! I am flaming angry at what has been dumped here! The Clorox bottles! The fast food wrappers! All these damned cigarette butts!"

"And the orange peels! And the old refrigerators!" I yelled.

"The Coke cans! The syringes! I'm mad as hell!" Dee yelled.

The goats were alarmed by all this shouting. They got quiet and still and then drifted toward and behind Nelda, who was silent.

"And I'm tired of the hate! Oh, am I tired of the hate! The way we all seek out the undesirables to dump our garbage onto."

"Me, too!" I loved this exuberance. "I'm mad as hell, too!"

"We're teaching you bad words," Dee said, her voice more hushed.

"I won't use them when I'm not with you," I promised. "I know better than that."

"You're a sharp cookie, Girl!" Dee said, and we continued our tirade as we walked up the mountain. Ester and Nelda got into it, too. We stormed and raged each time we saw one of the garbage dumps, until finally we were reduced to laughter.

The laughter and the anger were like companion logs helping each other burn even brighter. It was then I came to know this: that although hatred does not heal, anger does, if it is not infused with hate. Anger keeps us in touch with life and with hope. Without anger we are sunk.

Anger is a flow of life energy, a path of caring about what happens to yourself and to the earth. Well tended, that care intensifies to love.

By the time we reached the cabin, we were like flaming torches of life, laughing and raging until the fuel was spent and the coals of love lulled us into a more peaceful state.

After this, Dee changed. Don't get me wrong, she was still angry when she found a fresh pile of garbage. But she didn't swear under her breath while we logged. Ester always logged Dee as well as the dumped garbage after this, and I always pinned the note on Dee's shirt above her heart:

One old woman,

short and plump,

flaming hair

Once she had five such snips of paper pinned to her shirt before we got to the cabin. Each one seemed to bring more substance to Dee. She grew larger and, paradoxically, more content once Ester started logging her.

So when she rose full and brilliant as the harvest moon over the eastern ridge and offered the deputy the mail she'd collected from the pile just before the last curve, he studied her as if for the first time. "You might be interested in this," she said simply. And to everyone's amazement, he followed up. The next morning a couple was cleaning up the pile and stuffing it into black garbage bags.

That evening we talked about this interesting turn of events. I said maybe Dee had finally accepted that it was her job to be angry, but to not be so hateful about it.

"Maybe it's Dee's way of praying," Nelda smiled.

"Maybe so," Dee said quietly, not arguing with Nelda's nonsense this time.

SOPHIA, TELL ME THE ACCIDENT STORY.

That fateful afternoon I arrived at the cabin to find Nelda working on the goat pen. I could see Ester dozing in her rocker inside the open cabin door. Dee was not there. Nelda said she had gone to town alone because Ester was under the weather from a cold she had caught, and Nelda had stayed home to work on the goat pen. But I also suspect she wanted to look after Ester.

The acacia was in bloom, the air sweet and promising, and that scent has ever since been a poignant reminder of what happened next. The goats were plump from an afternoon of foraging fresh green grasses. Each one in turn inspected Nelda's work, trying to make away with a piece of wood or a paper wrapper, and then wandered off to doze on the porch near Ester. Nelda said they loved to doze almost as much as Ester did, and that they were probably frisking about in their daydreams looking for the next place to browse. This made me laugh. I could imagine their goat dream bodies frolicking about the new oak seedlings, leaping high, then clicking hind heels together and hightailing it back to wake up and get busy.

"Sophia, would you milk Natalie for me?" Nelda called. "Dee will be home soon—you didn't see her, did you?—and it will be time to make supper. I need to finish up here."

I had just learned to milk Natalie, or rather Natalie had just begun to allow me to do it. First I got a handful of molate fescue grass, her favorite, and then I fastened a leash to her collar and tied her to a small post near the goat pen. As she ate, I gently pulled the teats in a rhythm I had learned from Nelda. The milk spurted into a small stainless steel bucket that we used only for this purpose. We used this milk for our supper and any extra Nelda made into cheese. The squirting of the milk in the pail, the sweetness of the air, and the fading warmth of the afternoon sun, lulled me into quietude. Before I knew it, the sun was below the redwoods to the west.

"Sophia, stay with Ester. I'm going to check on Dee. She should have been back a while ago." Nelda's voice jarred me back to my senses. She was already walking down the path.

Nelda was gone a long time. The goats became still, standing in their pen and staring at me. At some point came the screaming of a siren, but I still wasn't worried. I rubbed the ridges of the goats' backs. They didn't move.

And Ester. Ester woke as Nelda left, but she sat in her rocker and rocked, not speaking. I remember the creaking of the rocker as I sat on the steps near her. Gradually the quiet boredom grew into an anxiety that I couldn't name. *When would they get back?* I remember the aluminum-colored sky after the sun set. I sat on the porch a long while, then I fed the goats their evening ration of sweet mix. They pepped up for that, but then went back to staring, just like me.

About the time I could see more than a few stars, I saw Nelda's flashlight coming back up the path. I was relieved, until I saw that she was alone. "Where's Dee?" I blurted out.

Nelda said nothing. Boris called to her, and then Natalie, and Tarquin. It was dark and I couldn't see at first that her eyes were red and swollen, her face wet.

Ester came to the door behind me. She said nothing.

"I have terrible news," Nelda said, and then her voice broke into sobs. I took her hand and pulled her to the porch.

"Sit down, Nelda," I said. Nelda let me pull her down on the step. Her head sunk into her lap as her shoulders heaved.

"What is it, honey?" Ester said in her soft voice. "What horrible thing has happened?" She had come forward and was sitting on the step beside Nelda. I kept thinking I felt Dee with us, too, but kept reminding myself that Dee didn't come back with Nelda.

"There's been an accident," Nelda said. "On the road. Where we've so often logged those dumpers. Dee was hit. She's gone! Ester, Dee is gone! They hit her and then drove off. She was dead when I got there. I walked to a neighbor's house and we called the ambulance. But she was dead."

I sat there numb and silent, not knowing that I was in shock, not even when the trembling started. I tried to think only of the waning moon, to cling to the lingering scent of the sun on the warmed earth. Yet noticing this beauty led me right back to what I could not escape: who was present and who was not.

We sat there a long time. Darkness wrapped us in coldness, and I got Ester her woolen shawl. When we went into the cabin, I felt sick to my stomach. I could not cry and didn't understand why. I kept thinking Dee was there. I kept seeing her out of the corner of my eye. Sometime much later, Nelda walked me down the mountain. The next morning I went back up almost as soon as it was light. Nelda was already dressed. She said she was going into town to see about the arrangements for Dee. Dee's son lived somewhere in southern California. He must be notified, she said, and would I stay with Ester and the goats.

Those days were a blur to me. I think it was the third evening that Nelda returned worn and tired, saying that the police had located and notified the son through driver's license records. She said that she had no idea what was to become of Dee's body.

"Maybe he'll let us bury her," I said.

"It's not our worry," Ester said. "Let her son make peace with his mother's body."

"The police say that it's up to him to notify us what the arrangements are," Nelda said. "And by law they can't hand out his whereabouts."

"But how will we know?" I asked. "Dee would want us to know!"

"We'll grieve Dee in the way she would want us to," Nelda said.

The next morning we walked to that spot where Dee had died. The dust on the road was obviously disturbed and darkly stained in one spot. There were still any number of tire tracks from ambulances and police cars, and somewhere beneath all that, tracks of the vehicle, probably a pickup, that had rounded the corner too fast and hit a small old woman in the road and then kept right on going.

The darkened spot was toward the right side of the road. Ester pulled her notebook out of her pocket and, standing in the tracks on the dirt road, began to log. I had gotten used to her logging almost everything that we came across, but I wasn't expecting this. When she handed me the note to pin up, I read it aloud slowly.

One pool of dried blood
Stained clay

No one said anything for a while. Finally, Nelda broke the silence. "If Dee was here, and I think that she just might be, she would have something to say."

"She'd be pissed," I said.

"She'd say, watch your English, Girl!" Nelda laughed.

"She'd say, sometimes there's just no other word that quite hits the spot," I countered, "and I think Dee would say, 'God damn it all, I'm pissed about this!'" I said this much louder than I ever imagined, and I was shocked to hear my throat begin releasing other sounds, too.

I grabbed Nelda and sobbed a long time. Nelda cried, too, and so did Ester. Nelda smoothed my hair and pretty soon the crying stopped.

"Dee was such a fighter," Ester said. "I am going to miss her. Such a way for a fighter to go."

"She died in the line of duty," I said, and I cried some more.

"Not the worst way to go," Nelda added. "Maybe the only way for Dee."

This made us all cry some more.

And so began my grieving of Dee, which is what precipitated the next part of the story. Once I started grieving, I just couldn't stop. I didn't want to go to school. Nelda insisted I should go. She said the school would notice if I wasn't there.

But I couldn't. I hid in the forest during the school day or laid on my stomach in the meadows where we often grazed the goats, letting the sun and the earth wrap me in their love, trying to heal the pain in my heart. Nelda knew, and she tried to intervene. She would ask me about school that day, her eyes wry and knowing. I said nothing because I didn't want to lie.

I had missed two weeks of school when I met Ma one morning just as I was preparing to leave the house for Huckleberry Mountain.

"Where the hell are you going," she said.

"School," I answered, surprised to see her up.

"Like you went yesterday?" she yelled. "What are you trying to do to me, child? Get me in big trouble? You haven't been going to school at all. They called me yesterday."

I said nothing. I was stunned. I had learned to flow around Ma, so I almost never had this kind of confrontation with her.

"Where've you been, goddamn it?"

I said nothing. Then from behind her I saw her latest boyfriend come out of the bedroom. "Answer your ma," he said.

I wasn't about to take orders from a strange man. I stared at him as if he were a pest who'd just pulled my hair.

"I said, answer your ma!" he yelled, grabbing my arm.

I wasn't used to this kind of treatment, and I wasn't about to get used to it, either. So I looked him in the eye and said, "Let go of my arm."

I don't remember much of what happened next. Memory softens times like this. I do remember the stinging jolt of a slap that knocked me flat, and I remember that the slaps just kept coming. I remember the smooth golden finish of the Douglas fir floorboards, of feeling the hint of splinteriness with my fingers. In time the man and my mother were yelling, and then he left the house.

I lay on the floor crying. I may even have gone to sleep. Suddenly I was roused by someone softly touching my hair. I thought at first that it was Ma, because she was the only one there, but then I heard Dee's voice say, *Goddamned mother fucking bastard!*

I looked up quickly, expecting to see Dee. The room was still, although a little disheveled from the ruckus, and no one was there. There were only the sounds of Ma crying in the bedroom.

"Dee!" I said, almost involuntarily, and I heard her voice again. *I'm well, Sophie. Don't worry about me anymore, I'm well. Now you get on with things.* A calmness came that I hadn't felt in a long time.

After a while Ma helped me get dressed. She was gentler than I've ever known her to be. The red sore spots on my arms and legs and chest and back were turning purple. She put a long-sleeved turtleneck on me and told me to not take it off. She helped me put on slacks that covered my legs. My face was bruised only a little.

"If anyone asks, tell them that you fell while you were playing." Then she took me to school. She didn't go in, and that was the last time I was with her.

I was still dazed. By recess the teacher had taken me to the nurse, who made me take off the turtleneck and then called the authorities. I told them I had fallen. They took me to a doctor. A kind woman interviewed me about my life, asking about Ma. There was almost nothing I could tell her. How could I explain that my real home was with Nelda and Ester and Dee and the goats, that I had all I needed with these Goat Women, so I didn't need Ma anymore?

This woman would never understand, I knew that from the way she took notes on the paper in front of her. She was logging me! I told her a neighbor was taking care of me. She wanted the address but I didn't know the address. She wanted the phone number but Nelda didn't have a phone. I knew she thought I was making all this up to protect Ma, just like I was making up the story about the bruises.

She went to Ma's house and found no food in the refrigerator, only beer. I had a history of not attending school. Therefore I wasn't being cared for, she decided, and I was to be taken to the dependent unit at Child Protective Services in the city an hour away.

Of course I panicked when I heard this. I had to get to Nelda and Ester! They'd be worried sick about me. When the woman loaded me into her car to drive me off, I felt numb with despair.

But just as we stopped at the red light on our way out of town, I heard Dee's voice. *Now, Girl!* she said, and without a thought I jumped out of the car and ran for my life. I had been so compliant up to now that this was the last thing the woman expected. She was so startled that I got quite a head start.

This way! Dee's voice said, and I took off in the direction opposite from Huckleberry Mountain. I ran around a corner and into a store, waiting to see which way the woman would go. I could just see her car from the front window, as she pulled the car over and ran back to the sidewalk she had seen me disappear down.

I walked calmly through the store, greeting the clerk in what I thought was a relaxed ten-year-old way. My life depended on keeping my head now. I walked out the door on the other side of the store, knowing I had only a short time to make it up Huckleberry Mountain. I knew the woman would call the sheriff, and soon they'd all be looking for me.

Nelda would know what to do. I walked casually and confidently along a walk leading to an alley, at which point I ran into a sheriff's deputy. I couldn't let him see me heading this way. *Ask him about the bus toward Jenner and the coast,* Dee's voice said. Jenner was the opposite direction from the dependent unit. I walked up to the deputy who was making some notes on a pad. "Excuse me, sir, would you tell me which side of the street I can catch the bus to the ocean?"

The deputy was the kind of man I wish Ma had gotten involved with, sweet and strong. "Right over there, in front of Safeway," he said.

"Thanks," I said, and skipped off.

Go toward Safeway. Take the alley to the right of the bus stop. Then high-tail it up the mountain. Now Get!" Apparently, Dee still loved giving orders.

It made me laugh to hear Dee's voice. Just as I got to the alley, the bus came and stopped, blocking me from the deputy's view. Several people got off and several got on, including a couple of girls I knew from school. I casually walked until I got into the alley, and then I ran for all I was worth. Soon I was clear of the houses and in the forest. "Oh, thank you, Dee!" I said, but all was quiet. "Oh please, Mountain! Please Redwoods! Please Path! Help my feet find a safe passage up Mountain!"

I closed my eyes a moment to feel for the stars of Mountain. A slight breeze came and soothed my face. The path was somewhat overgrown, but I made good time. Somewhere about halfway to the top, I met Nelda, who was breathless. "Thank God, Sophia! What has happened? The goats suddenly went wild this morning, and when you didn't come after school, I knew something awful had happened … Oh my God! Sophia! Who did this to you?"

She held me a long time, kissing my bruises. I told her the story. I told her how Dee had come and helped me, and that Dee was alright. I told her about the woman from the authorities, and the deputy. Her face darkened, like the gathering clouds before a storm. "Let's go home," she said. "We have to think." And we walked slowly the rest of the way up the mountain, Nelda's hand warm and firm about my own.

16

TELL ME THE TIME YOU HID FROM THE DEPUTY AND ATE FLAMES.

Well, as you can imagine, we were paid a visit by the deputy before dark. I was in the goat pen when I heard him coming. We all knew that my time with Nelda, Ester, and the goats was limited, and I wanted to savor every last minute of it. I sat with the goats as they fought for my attention, which always made me laugh. Nelda was in the house with Ester when I heard the deputy thrashing through the brush. It was quite a little jaunt from the road up to Nelda's cabin, so I was glad for the advanced warning.

Quick, up here, Girl. I was coming to not think twice when I heard Dee's voice. I instantly hopped to my feet and climbed the coastal oak that grew behind the goats' shed. Its branches were thick and shielding, and in the darkening light I would not be seen.

Nelda met the deputy on the porch and invited him into the cabin. He was there for a while. I propped myself up in the crotch of a huge branch and felt my body relax. The bark was rough and scaly with lichens and tiny branches protruded and pressed my bruises, but as my body relaxed I could feel the tree's medicine enter me, and soon I was asleep.

I must not have slept for long. I heard the deputy on the porch, and Nelda's voice. "Well, give me this evening," she said. "I think I might be able to find her. I'll be in touch with you tomorrow."

"Good enough," the deputy answered. I could tell by his relaxed manner that Nelda had inspired his confidence. But her words cut me to the quick. *No, Nelda!* I wailed inside. *I want to stay with you.*

You know that would be impossible. They won't allow that, Girl. Hearing Dee's words made me cry.

The deputy disappeared down the path. Nelda walked over to the goat pen and stared up into the tree. "Come on down, Sophia. Let's put the goats to bed."

And so I did. Funny how things can suddenly be in sharper focus and bathed in new meaning. The way

Natalie's small stout legs held that egg of a body, and the warmth of her milk in the pail. The piercing call of an osprey overhead. The grassy smell of Boris' coat. The gleaming smoothness of Hornsby's horns, curved back, like twin crescent moons. It was okay if nothing else ever happened to me. This was enough forever.

"There's no way they will let me keep you," Nelda said as we started in. "I asked the deputy. He said there are regulations on the living space, and they would move you out of this community anyway. Away from your mother."

"My mother would be no problem."

"I know, Sophie, but they don't. The laws are to protect you, and they stick to the law."

"I hate the law," I said. Nelda hugged me.

That evening time seemed to just stop. There was no past or future. When Nelda and I got inside, Ester was in her chair rocking, her cheeks damp with tears. "Oh, Sophia!" she said, and grabbed my hand. I sat down beside her for a while.

Nelda was preparing supper. "Come, I have something to show you," she said. She stood beside the stove, stirring polenta. "Look here, in the pot, at this polenta I am cooking. Look carefully, do you see?"

I looked in the pot. The golden mixture erupted in occasional swellings which exploded into air. "What, Nelda?"

"Do you see how the stars we saw in the grass are also here in the polenta?" she asked.

I stared into the pot with unbelieving eyes. She was right. I didn't exactly see the stars, but I felt them. It was a feeling in my heart, in my soul. "Can I stir?" I asked.

She handed me the spoon, and I stirred, marveling at this beautiful thick golden pot of polenta that we were about to eat. Nelda stood beside me, cracking walnuts. "Want a piece?" she offered, smiling.

I opened my mouth as she laid it on my tongue. Slowly I chewed. Outside I heard the melancholy song of some night bird. The polenta bubbled.

Nelda soon had a tray filled with walnuts, which she roasted in the oven. We scooped spoonfuls of the polenta into bowls and sprinkled walnuts and goat cheese on the top.

We ate our last supper together slowly. Nelda let me bring Boris into the cabin for a while, and he lay at our feet, occasionally baaing. "He's singing a Goatsong," Nelda said.

As I listened, I felt Dee among us, sensed all that wasn't there and all that was. There was only the joy and the grief of the present. The familiar sound of Nelda's chair scooting across the wood floor as she pushed herself back from the table to get more polenta. The crack of the rocker as Ester moved back and forth, the silence caused by the lack of Dee's chatter. The smell of goat cheese and polenta and the dry woodiness of Nelda's cabin.

For the first time in my life, eating was a holy experience. The star nature of the polenta and walnuts erupted into pure essence of flame. When you eat, knowing this flame, you are deeply fed. A little is enough. This is the living food. And once you taste it, nothing can ever be the same again.

What I learned from the Goat Women is that the Fire comes in all kinds of packages. It comes in polenta and in zucchini, and in peas and corn, and it comes in wheat and grapes and spinach. In the end, it doesn't matter much what the package is, although you may think so at the time. Like, maybe you haven't yet acquired a taste for Brussels sprouts. But those little round heads are packages of star fire, too, just like the polenta, and it really doesn't take that much to fill you, once you know this. As long as what you eat has the fire inside, you are going to be alright.

17

SOPHIA, IS IT THAT WAY WITH MOTHERS, TOO?

I think so, Stace. I know now the Fire just wasn't in my mother. And she couldn't help it. But then, it didn't matter as much after I met the Goat Women. Through their loving, if unorthodox, attention, I thrived. And this sustained me when I was sent to my foster mother, away from Nelda and Ester, although at the time I thought my heart would break to leave them and the goats. Nelda showed me this secret, how to recognize the stars and know the flame within everything, and because she showed me, I could see my foster mother had a little of it. Once you are shown the stuff, you are almost home free.

18

DID YOU EVER SEE NELDA
AND ESTER AGAIN?

Not after Nelda took me down to the police station the next morning. As we left the cabin I said my goodbyes to the goats. Nelda clipped a few hairs from each goat and put them in a small pouch as soft as Natalie's udders. It's the pouch I still wear around my neck.

Then Ester walked out on the porch, carrying her pencil and notebook. I thought, *now she's going to log me, too.* But she didn't. Instead she put the notebook down there on the porch floor and the pencil on top of it, and she said, "Sophia, my logging is over. I have had enough of it. I love you, honey. God be with you." She hugged me a long time, and we cried.

I was sent far away. Too far. When I was old enough to get back to visit, there was a housing development where Nelda's cabin used to be. Only the goat barn remained, now

165

someone's garden shed, and the coastal oak, which had grown even larger.

No one knew what happened to Nelda and Ester, but there were rumors of wild goats seen occasionally on Huckleberry Mountain. I like to think they all went feral—Ester feral into the next world, I imagine, and Nelda and the goats into those hills and mountains north of Huckleberry. I sometimes imagine them all becoming part of the flame of those redwoods and mountains, part of the powerful whishing of osprey wings many feet over your head, part of the last song of the creek before summer dryness sets in. I smell them in the sweet scent of spring, and in the winter the wild winds bring intonations of their whereabouts.

I can still hear Dee's voice when things get really rough, and Ester's calm vision has visited me many times. And Nelda lives here in my heart. And sometimes I hear the tinkle of a bell and feel Boris and Natalie, Emily and Hornsby—and I remember the Goatsong, that melody that is almost too sweet to bear. And yet we must, if we are to live. It's all due to them, Stace, and I was one of them for a while, one of the Goat Women—the Goat Women of Huckleberry Mountain who brought me into life.

also by Patricia Damery

Snakes, a novel
ISBN 978-1-926715-13-1

Farming Soul: A Tale of Initiation
ISBN 978-1-926715-01-8

Made in the USA
Charleston, SC
07 October 2012